PLEASE DON'T GO

A PSYCHOLOGICAL THRILLER

H.K. CHRISTIE

KEEKSTAR MEDIA

This is a work of fiction. Names, characters, businesses, places, events and incidents are either the products of the author's imagination or used in a fictitious manner. Any resemblance to actual persons, living or dead, or actual events is purely coincidental.

Copyright © 2025 by H.K. Christie

Cover design by Odile Stamanne

All rights reserved.

No part of this book may be reproduced in any form or by any electronic or mechanical means, including information storage and retrieval systems, without written permission from the publisher, except for the use of brief quotations in a book review.

If you would like to use material from this book, prior written permission must be obtained by contacting the publisher at:

www.authorhkchristie.com

First edition: May 2025

ISBN: 978-1-953268-21-1

041725h

For all the Blockheads still Hangin' Tough.

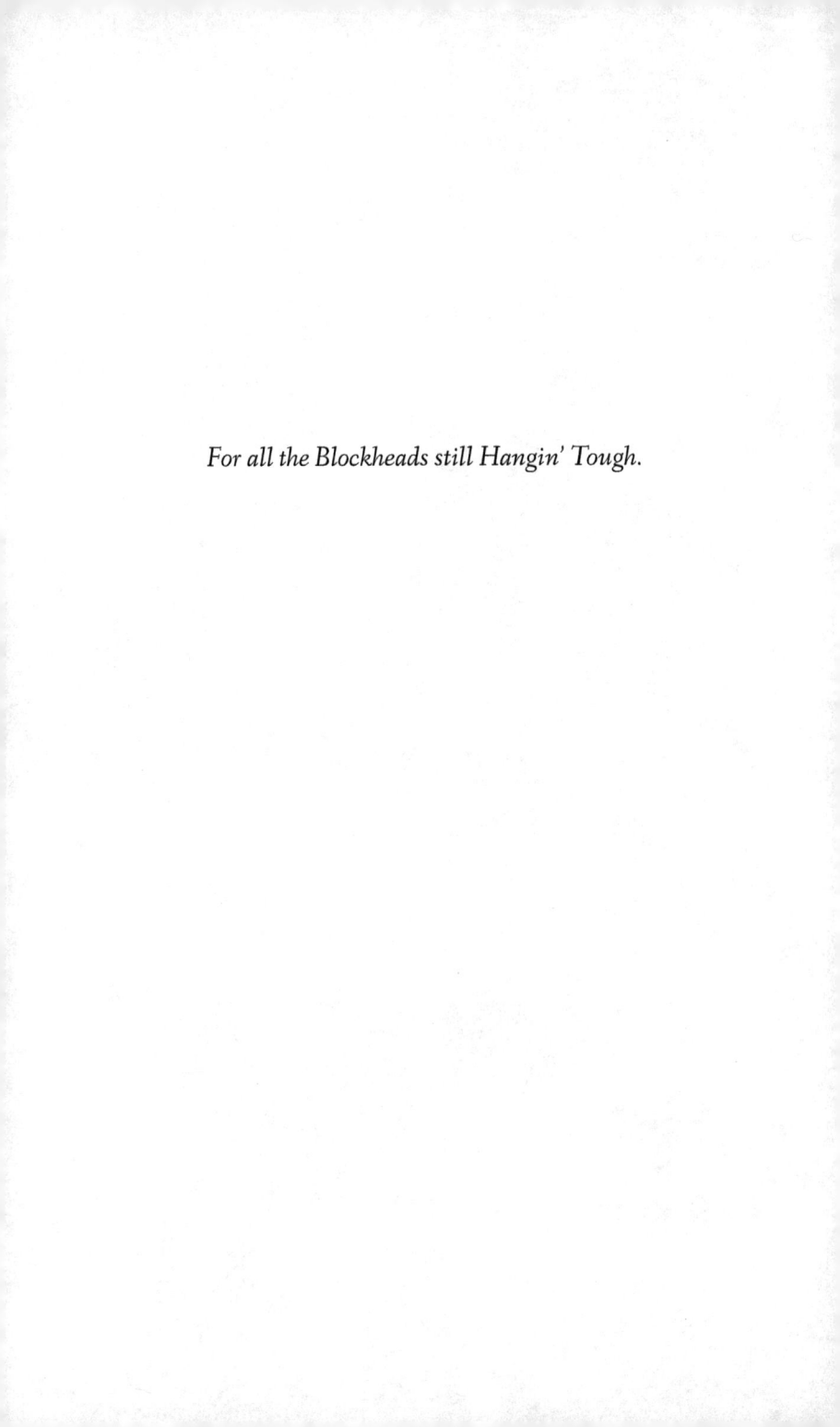

CHAPTER ONE

I DIDN'T PLAN to kill him, but I'm glad he's dead.

It's funny how there are moments in life you look back on—pivotal moments—that bring you exactly to where you are now. Decisions you make that seem insignificant at the time but drag you far from the path you think you're on. If someone told me a year ago that I'd be standing here, gun still warm in my hands, I would've laughed. But here I am, staring down at his lifeless body, a pool of blood spreading beneath him, and I can hardly reconcile the past me with the person I am now.

His face is twisted in horror, and his eyes are wide with surprise—frozen in that last, split-second realization that I'm capable of more than he thought. He underestimated me. This man thought I didn't have it in me to pull the trigger. He thought I was weak and breakable—incapable of fighting back.

That's where he went wrong. He wasn't unique. He wasn't the first to underestimate me. That's what I don't understand. What did I do or say that makes others believe I'm not strong and capable? Because I am.

My hands tremble as I lower the weapon. The scent of

gunpowder still lingers in the air, mixing with the metallic tang of blood. I step closer, my breath coming in shallow, uneven gasps. I nudge him with the tip of my boot, the leather pressing into his still chest. His body is motionless. I'm fairly certain he's dead, but I need to be sure.

His eyes—blank and staring—reflect nothing. The light in them is gone. But was there ever any light there to begin with? Or has he always been a soulless, hollow monster, walking around in human skin?

Regret washes over me, creeping up my spine. Not for the fact he's gone, but for the fact he's gone in an instant. He didn't suffer. Death is a mercy, and he doesn't deserve mercy. An easy way out is too kind for someone like him. He deserves more, so much more. He has gotten away with too much and has lived too long without consequences.

Rage, hot and all-consuming, still bubbles in my veins, refusing to die down. I imagine all the things I could have done if I'd planned this better. If I'd decided beforehand that he had to die, I would have made it last. Maybe a shot to the kneecap so he twisted in pain, begging me to stop. Pleading for a shred of decency. I wouldn't have given it to him. But I didn't look that far ahead. I should have, but killing him wasn't part of my plan.

When the shot rang out, and before I even registered what happened, he crumpled to the ground. The stillness that has followed feels unnatural, like the world itself has paused. One bullet ended him. His life has been extinguished so quickly and completely. I didn't expect that. The finality of it hits me hard, knocking the air from my lungs.

My mind spirals, thinking of the women he has wronged. The lives he has shattered. Maybe they'll want to know he's dead. Maybe there's some justice in that. But as I stand here, my body trembling, I can't shake the feeling that this might not just be the end of him but of me, too.

The sound of someone calling my name breaks through the chaos in my mind. It barely registers, muffled and distant against the roar in my head. I glance over my shoulder, and that's when the unthinkable crosses my mind.

Do I have to kill him, too?

CHAPTER TWO

6 WEEKS EARLIER

The door slams shut with a life-shattering bang. The sound screams through my empty apartment and into my being. I flinch, feeling something splinter deep inside me. I stand frozen, staring at the door that now separates us.

Does that closed door mark an end or a beginning? There's some old saying about a window opening when a door closes—but if that's true, why do I feel like I'm going to be sick?

A sharp pang twists in my stomach, the kind that comes from raw, unfiltered heartbreak. Even now, nearly a year later, one question still haunts me. Why doesn't he care about me anymore?

The thought slices through me like a dull blade. I gave Joe everything—my love and my devotion for more than a decade of my life—only for him to walk away as if none of it matters. As if I don't matter. He discards me as easily as a greasy fast-food bag, tossed aside after devouring the last French fry.

The thought of fries springs some not-so-great memories of our time together. It's as if I can still hear his casual, cutting remarks, disguised as concern for "our" health whenever I ate unhealthy foods. The way he eyed my plate when I indulged in fries, making offhand comments obviously directed at me. Memories of the last time springs to my mind.

He said, "Maybe we should start eating healthier."

I dropped the burger onto my plate and said, "Are you saying I'm fat?"

"No, of course not. Don't be crazy, Jessica."

There it was, that word again—crazy. I balled my fists and snapped, "I'm not crazy!" And then I stormed off.

By that point in our relationship, I'd gained twenty pounds, but it wasn't like he was exactly skinny either. Still, I was a woman—his wife. My worth, in his eyes, was conditional—tied to numbers on a scale, to my appearance, to how well I fit into his perfect, polished world. When we met, I thought he was the perfect guy, and I was the luckiest girl in the world. More like the biggest *fool*.

Did he ever really love me? Or was I just a placeholder until something shinier, newer, better came along? The memory flashes me back to nearly one year earlier.

Over a dinner I had prepared for him, he said, "This is really hard, Jessica, so I'm just going to come out and say it. I've met someone."

"What do you mean, you've met someone?"

"It wasn't planned. We're in love. I'm so sorry."

I drifted into some other place and could hardly decipher his words, but it basically amounted to him finally understanding what real—passionate—love felt like. As if the past decade of our life together wasn't real. As if I was nothing more than a trial run before he found *her*.

I finally snapped out of the shock and said, "So, what you're saying is you never really love me?"

In that condescending tone of his, he said, "I didn't know what love was back then. We'd been dating for two years. I was getting pressure from my parents to settle down and start a family. Getting married seemed like the right thing to do."

I thought: *The right thing to do.* That would have been useful information before I said yes to the princess cut diamond ring and all the promises he made with it—before I built my world and identity around him.

Fury blurred my thoughts, and that was when the screaming started. The crying. And finally, the begging. "Please don't do this. Don't leave me. You're just going to throw away ten years together?"

"I'm sorry, Jessica. I really am. You'll find someone new. Someone perfect for you. I want that for you. I wish you the best."

He wished me the best? The rage returned. "Who is she?"

"You don't know her."

"How old is she?"

He wouldn't meet my gaze.

"How old is she?" I asked again.

"Twenty-five."

All I could do to keep from breaking was laugh. "Oh, I get it! You're having a midlife crisis! Why didn't you say so? We can work through this."

Silence filled the room, and I swear it was a full minute later when he said, "She's pregnant. I'm so sorry." His voice cracked. His eyes glistened with the perfect amount of remorse.

The air was knocked out of me. After all the months of IVF and heartbreaking disappointment, he simply went and found someone to give him what I couldn't. In the moment, I hated him. I suspected he wasn't sorry for breaking his vows—or me. He was only sorry to be labeled the villain. A man who dropped his first wife for a woman half his age whom he'd knocked up. He became a cliché.

The anger turned into deep sadness, and that was when the

tears returned. There was no working through a pregnant mistress. He'd destroyed me. The conversation ended, and I packed up my things.

I wipe my fresh tears. A year later, he has everything—a new woman, a baby, our house, and all our plans for the future—while I'm left with this sterile, impersonal apartment and a pile of boxes that contain the last remnants of my old life.

He came by, not to check on me, not to see how I'm holding up since he blew up my life. No, he only came by to drop off the things I left in *his* house. My boxes cluttered his garage and took up space that his new little family needs.

I glance at the boxes stacked neatly in the corner. I'm just another thing he needed to get rid of—a thing he no longer has use for.

On the outside, I pretend I'm relieved to be free of him. To coworkers and friends who ask how I'm doing, I say stupid things like, "I'm doing great!" and "I can't wait for a fresh start." *Lies.* Beneath the façade, I am hollow. I go through the motions—wake up, shower, work, repeat—each day bleeding into the next, gray and lifeless.

I used to think my life was on track. That I found the one person who truly saw me. Joe swept me off my feet with his confidence, his charm, and his maturity. He was older and made me feel beautiful and desirable. At first, it was intoxicating. Now, I see him for what he is—a coward. A fraud. How did I ever believe anything he said?

Maybe I'll feel excited about starting over and taking charge of my life once the dull ache in my chest eases up. Once I feel like life has something left for me.

I slide down the wall, plop myself on the cold tile, and stare at the boxes he left. Written in faded Sharpie, the word "Memorabilia" labels the side of the most worn-out box. I have no idea what's in it.

A flicker of something stirs inside me—curiosity. I push myself upright and hurry into the kitchen to grab a box cutter from my utility drawer. Back in the living room, my fingers tremble slightly as I slice through the tape, the sound oddly satisfying. One quick swipe, and the flaps pop open.

I peer inside—and for the first time in a year, my lips curve into a genuine smile and I remember there was a time I was truly happy. A time I felt like I belonged. A time before Joe. A time I nearly forgot—or perhaps *tried* to forget.

CHAPTER THREE

Pushing away the dark thoughts, I stand wide-eyed. I can't believe I still have it. My New Soundz tour jacket from more than two decades earlier. I run my fingers over the worn, slightly faded fabric, feeling a surge of nostalgia so intense it makes my chest ache. It is my prized possession from childhood —a time when all I could think about was the New Soundz and how much I loved all five band members. As a young teen, they weren't just a band to me. They were my escape, my obsession, my everything.

And it wasn't just them that made my life so full of joy. I had friends back then—real friends. My ride-or-die—my best friend in the entire world—was Rochelle. Since the day we met, an unspeakable bond had connected us.

Before that life went away, all we could talk about, all we could think about, was the New Soundz and our future marriages to two of the band members. We knew every word to every song and every detail about their lives that we could find in magazines and online. We spent our afternoons watching their music videos, trading collectible cards, and daydreaming about what it would be like to meet them.

Older, and a little wiser, I realize that what the New Soundz gave us was more than entertainment. They provided hope and something to cling to in a world that is often unkind.

I remember meeting Rochelle so clearly despite the fact it's been twenty-two years. It was the first day of eighth grade, and I didn't know anybody at the middle school. I was the new kid—*again*. At thirteen years old, I had already attended six different schools. You'd think I would have gotten used to it by that point and become adept at making new friends, but I wasn't. I was shy, painfully so, and terrified of meeting new people. Most kids my age seemed fearless, but not me. I kept to myself, guarded and closed off, afraid that if someone got too close, they'd learn the truth about me. But then I met Rochelle, and everything changed.

I was sitting in homeroom, hunched over my desk with a swirl of anxiety brewing in my stomach as I doodled hearts and wrote "I heart New Soundz" over and over in my notebook. Suddenly, the desk next to mine scraped across the floor and pushed up against me. I glanced over and saw a girl with long brown hair, a dusting of freckles, and oversized glasses that looked too big for her face. She leaned in with wide, excited eyes, and said, "Oh my gosh, do you love the New Soundz?"

My heart skipped. Did I love the New Soundz? Obsessed didn't even cover it. They were my everything. I played their songs over and over again on my CD player until the lettering on the label wore out and the words were barely legible. I turned to her and nodded. "I love them."

"Me too! I'm Rochelle," she said, flashing me a grin and sticking out her hand to shake mine.

I hesitated for a moment, then shook her hand, feeling something like hope bloom inside me. "I'm Jessica."

"Where are you from?"

I sighed internally. It was a question I got a lot, and my answer always felt like a half-truth. "Recently? From Concord."

"Recently?"

"We kind of move around a lot," I said, trying to sound nonchalant, but I was secretly begging the universe that Rochelle wouldn't ask any follow-up questions.

With a shrug, she said, "Oh, that's cool." She pushed up her glasses. "So, you don't know anybody here?"

"No."

Before she could respond, the bell rang, and the teacher called out, "Everyone settle down. Time for class."

Rochelle turned back to me, her face bright with a smile. "Meet me after class, OK?"

And right then, in that small moment, I knew Rochelle would change my world. And she did. She really did.

CHAPTER FOUR

I LIFT the jacket out of the box, my hands trembling slightly as the memories flood back. The iconic white New Soundz logo against the black fabric glints under the dim light of my apartment, and my heart clenches. Beneath the jacket, I immediately spot an old photo album. Based on the happy face sticker on the front, I know it's the scrapbook I put together with Rochelle, page by painstaking page, during the happiest days of my childhood—strike that—the only happy times in my childhood.

I hurry to my sofa and carefully place the jacket over the back to prominently display the New Soundz logo. It is like giving a place of honor to an old, beloved friend. I rush back to the box and grab the scrapbook, my fingers already itching to turn the pages. I collapse onto the couch and flip open the lid, the rush of emotions hitting me hard. Right there, on the first page, are four ticket stubs from all the concerts Rochelle and I attended together.

Thinking back to that first concert, a pang of bittersweet nostalgia washes over me. Rochelle and I had only recently become friends, bonded instantly over our shared love for the boy band. But after only a few months, Rochelle's family treated me like one of their own. Every day after school, Rochelle and I walked to her house and hung out in her bedroom. Her mother always offered snacks and then would leave us to talk about boys and music. They even took me out to dinner a few times and never asked me to pay.

And then it happened—the New Soundz announced they were touring in the Bay Area. Rochelle and I screamed with excitement and insisted we had to go. The next day at school, Rochelle ran up to me with glee in her eyes. "Oh my gosh! I have the best news ever. My mom tells me that she's willing to camp out with us to buy our tickets to the concert. Your mom is invited too, if she wants to come."

It sounded like good news, but I didn't quite understand. Didn't we just call up and buy tickets? "Where would we camp out?"

"Outside the record store, where they sell the tickets. Mom says that when she was young, she used to do it all the time. She says it's so fun. Like the most fun. Two days before the tickets go on sale, we bring snacks and our sleeping bags; it's like going camping. By doing that, we can make sure we get tickets before they sell out and we'll get the best seats. I'm super psyched. We're going to see the New Soundz, Jess!"

It sounded so great, and the New Soundz were the biggest band, after all. It was smart of her mom to think ahead. Rochelle was so lucky to have a mom like Tina. I said, "Awesome! After school, I'll ask my mom if it's okay." We jumped up and down and hugged.

Chuckling at the memory, I think today we would have been hunched over our computers trying to score a code to buy the tickets on the internet, as opposed to packing for a campout.

My smile fades as I remember the embarrassment I felt when I had to tell Rochelle I couldn't go to the concert. The memory surfaces vividly. *Another heartbreak.*

After I told my mom about the concert invitation and campout, her answer was the same as it always was with anything I wanted to do or buy. With a sneer, she said, "How are you gonna pay for that? We don't have money for that."

Her words stung, cutting through my joy, and I nodded, trying to hold back the tears that burned in my eyes. Before I could argue, she said, "Oh, great. Here comes the waterworks again."

With disappointment and fury, I ran to my and my sister's room and flung myself onto the bed. I pounded at the mattress as hot tears streamed down my face while mumbling, "It's not fair!"

At school the next day, I told Rochelle, my voice thick with shame, that I couldn't go. I'd never felt so humiliated. I wanted to sink into the floor and disappear, terrified that Rochelle would decide I wasn't worth being friends with after all.

The truth was, my family had some money. But my mom and her boyfriend earmarked it for booze, drugs, or whatever *they* wanted. Not for me. Not for my little sister, Lucy. I wanted to scream at them, to ask why our lives had to revolve around their needs, their vices. Maybe if they didn't waste money on those things, our lives could have been different. Or maybe things would have been worse. Could things have been worse? Things can *always* be worse.

As an adult, on a good day, I like to think my mom and dad did their best, but that rationale might just be to make myself feel better—an attempt to prove to myself that my parents actually loved me. But even as a child, I wondered why they had kids if they didn't want to take care of them. Why be parents if they couldn't do anything more than just make us?

My therapist pointed out I was neglected and lived in a traumatic environment, and that makes me a survivor. I think she says it to make me feel proud or strong, but it just makes me feel more sad.

It wasn't until that moment in my therapist's office that I realized the New Soundz and Rochelle had been my lifeline, my escape from a family that felt more like a punishment than a source of love and safety.

When I told Rochelle I couldn't afford the concert ticket, she went home that night and told her mom. The next day at school, she ran up to me, her face beaming with excitement once again. "My mom says she doesn't want you to pay! She says it's a Christmas present!"

I was stunned by their kindness. It was one of the first times I felt that someone really cared about me. *And* that they pitied me.

That was the beginning.

The New Soundz and Rochelle became my escape from reality. Through the music and Rochelle and our shared obsession, I found something beautiful to cling to, something full of hope, love, and a sense of belonging.

Staring down at the concert tickets, I flash back to that very first concert together, the way we screamed until we lost our voices, cried when the boys danced and sang, hugged each other tight, and held hands, feeling the energy of the crowd. The entire stadium full of fans moved as one, and for the first time in my life, I felt like I truly belonged and understood what happiness felt like.

An ache in my heart reminds me of how fleeting it all is. Despite the joy we shared—four concerts, countless sleepovers, camping out for tickets, hours of singing and dancing in her bedroom, and dreams of one day marrying one of the band members—it all came to an abrupt and painful end. The fantasy we created to shield ourselves from reality didn't last forever.

Like my marriage, it was over so quickly it feels like maybe it never happened at all.

CHAPTER FIVE

It's another Mental Monday, my term for my every-other-week therapy session. I started up with Wanda when I hit thirty—knowing that I could use someone to talk to about all my troubles that no one around me could relate to. Someone to help me forget my past—to stop the nightmares. To deal with my present—at the time not being able to conceive and the strain it put between Joe and me. I was sure with therapy my worries would disappear, the stress would melt away, and I'd soon have a baby.

I learned pretty quick that therapy isn't about forgetting at all. It's about working through it. For the first year, I poured myself into it. The work was brutal. Being honest with my past trauma was like reliving the worst times of my life. The nightmares increased, and I was more stressed than ever. After a year, I still hadn't told her everything but chose to stop diving into all the dark parts of my past. Considering it's five years later and I have no child and no husband, I have to ask, was it all for nothing?

Settled into the comfy chair across from my therapist, I try to relax. Wavy Wanda is what I call her in my head because she waves her hands a lot when she talks—her hands moving in swooping arcs, her head bobbing as if in sync with music only she can hear. Our conversation topics have shifted through the years from childhood trauma to infertility to divorce to work and the concept of happiness. I'm not sure any of the sessions have helped. I'm starting to think it's simply a place to have someone who is forced to listen to all my thoughts and problems.

Wanda studies me. Her hands still for the moment, her expression a mask of patience. I don't know if she truly understands me anymore. Perhaps because I stopped being totally honest with her. Even I am tired of hearing my sad stories. Instead of getting into the real stuff, I play the part of a positive person ready for my next chapter. *Barf*. It's all an act. But therapists have to believe what you tell them, right? All they have to go on is your word. Say "I'm fine," and they have to accept it. Say "I'm moving on," and they nod like they believe you. But can Wanda see through it?

"How have things been the past few weeks?" she asks.

"Pretty good," I say. "Joe came by last night with a few boxes of mine that he found in his garage."

Wanda tilts her head. "What are in the boxes? Why did he have them?"

It's a legitimate question. Why were they still there, considering I moved out of our home—no, strike that—*his* home a year ago. Even my mother, with all her flaws, warned me that Joe should add me to the deed to the house after we were married. I thought it was unnecessary because I trusted him. Joe was fifteen years older, more established, and bought the home before we were married. After we were married, he insisted it was our house and not to worry about the unlikely what-ifs. And when I told Joe my mother had recommended it, he said she was just a bitter old woman who had no experience with healthy relationships. That may be, but she was right. I *really* hate that she was right.

"They're old boxes," I say. "He and his fiancée were cleaning out the garage and stumbled upon them. He was kind enough to drop them off."

Wanda's eyebrows lift slightly. "What's inside the boxes?"

"I haven't finished going through them. But I opened one. It has band memorabilia—things I collected back when I was a teen." My mind drifts back to those memories of Rochelle and that time. In those years, I had an escape from my life. It was as if when I was with her, fangirling over the New Soundz, I could escape my childhood. I had two lives. There was the life with chaos and shame, and then there was this other, bright life where I could pretend that the other world didn't exist. With Rochelle, I could compartmentalize, pretend I was someone bigger and better than just a sad, poor girl from a broken, drug-infested home. What I would give to have an escape like that again.

"You're not curious about the rest?"

"I'll get to them."

"How did you feel about Joe dropping off the boxes?"

Heartbroken. Empty. Angry. "It was weird to see him in my new apartment. He's never been over before."

"How does that make you feel to see him in your new space?"

Typical question. "How does that make you feel?" Sometimes, I imagine recording her and just playing the question back to myself over and over. Do they dedicate entire courses in medical school to that phrase?

"I guess it feels final," I say. "Like he's really done with me."

"That must be very hurtful to you."

"It was more hurtful when he left me for his pregnant twenty-five-year-old girlfriend," I say, bitterness creeping into my tone. Not that I am a spinster at thirty-five. But c'mon. He left me for a Gen Z-er?

Wanda nods, making a note on her notepad, her pen scratching quietly in the space between us. "Do you want to talk about those feelings?"

I think, *No, not really*. I would rather scream and stab him and his little girlfriend until the life drains out of them. Maybe then they would understand what they did to me. Instead of sharing those thoughts, I simply shake my head.

"How are you coping? It's been almost a year, and your divorce is just about final, right?"

"I'm moving on—keeping busy."

Wanda tilts her head again, her signature move when she wants to press further. "How are you keeping busy? Are you doing things outside of work? Are you meeting up with friends?"

Friends. The word stings more than it should. Nobody really knows how to talk to me anymore, and they all have their own lives filling up their space. It isn't their fault. They have young children and happy marriages. I am simply the divorced, barren thirty-something who can't smile without a half a bottle of chardonnay in me. My friends simply can't relate. Being around them only makes me feel more alone. Like an outsider.

Why am I the only one who can't give my husband a child or joy or the love he wants? Maybe I'm not lovable. Hasn't the universe shown me this time and time again?

I force a smile. "Well, we have our company party coming up, so that should be fun. I hear they're doing a casino night." My company doesn't want to pay the holiday rates and does the annual party in the Spring.

"That sounds fun," Wanda says, her eyes lighting up. "Are you looking forward to it?"

"Yeah, I think it's going to be great." The words come out flat, the same line I gave my boss.

In truth, I dread it. Spending more time with my coworkers,

putting on a fake smile while pretending to care about our department's latest initiatives—it all feels exhausting. Most of the people I work with are polite, but not exactly engaging. I chose a career in IT, after all. For work, I mostly stay behind a computer, creating user interfaces and landing pages. *I love computers.* They never disappoint me, and they always perform as they're programmed.

"That's great," Wanda says. "It seems like you're really making progress."

Progress. If only she knew that every line I feed her is hollow, and I feel like a husk of a person. Yet I keep coming to these sessions, clinging to some shred of hope that one day I'll be fixed. I have to go on, don't I? I found happiness once. Surely, I can find it again. But how? Everyone I have ever loved has left me, just like Joe.

"Any trips coming up? I know how you like to travel."

In my early twenties, my girlfriends and I traveled all over the world exploring new countries and cities. *Living out loud.* That was before we all got married and they had children. In hindsight, my twenties, before I ever met Joe, are full of more happiness than a single year spent with him. Why did I not realize it before? Am I as big a fraud as Joe—doing the things I think I am supposed to do, even if I am never truly happy?

"Nothing yet," I say, trying to sound upbeat. "But I'm definitely considering it."

I am not.

"Let's create a plan for the next few weeks. Keep you on the positive track that you're on."

How can she not see that I am barely holding it together and that all of my progress is a lie? Why don't I tell her the truth? Help her—help me—get fixed. Instead, I keep quiet, nodding along, playing the part of someone who is getting better.

We come up with three bullet points for "homework," as

Wavy Wanda calls it. One is to try something new that I've never done before. It is supposed to break me out of the mundane routine I'm living in.

What new thing can I do? No idea. The other is to take daily walks since I haven't stepped into a gym since I split from Joe. And last, to tell my mother and sister I am getting divorced —she insists it's part of healing and moving on. Most years I only see them at Christmas, if at all. So why would I call them up to tell them I failed at being a wife and mother? It isn't likely I'll do any of my homework, but I force another smile and say goodbye.

Leaving her office, I step into the cold, indifferent world and head back to my cubicle.

INSIDE THE CUBE FARM, my coworkers greet me with their annoyingly polite smiles, every one of them so controlled, so contained. Maybe they're all dying inside, too. Maybe we all are. Maybe that's why nobody can see my pain—they're too busy fighting their own.

My thoughts linger back to my therapy session and how I told Wanda I was going to try something new. I'd pretended I would, but now I think I should. I didn't always want to be the sad, lonely girl. The one with nothing to live for. *I can't go back to that dark place.* Maybe I just need to loosen up. I could go out, have a drink, or two, or three. Joe used to hate when I drank too much. He'd say I got silly and loud. But maybe I need to be silly and loud. Maybe I need to live out loud once again and no longer be the timid little mouse I had become.

For too long, I lived a restrained life, suffocating under expectations that aren't mine. Trying to be perfect and how I think Joe wanted me to be. I can finally be free. The thought feels pivotal, electric.

Perhaps Wanda is worth her hourly rate, after all.

Something clicks, and I think maybe I can be someone new—or maybe rediscover the person I once was, the girl who once full of life and dreams. Like when I was with Rochelle and singing along to the New Soundz. I was only a teen back then, but I was suddenly and strangely feeling confident I could be that way again.

I picture Joe with his tucked-in, button-down plaid shirts, his dark denim, his shiny Italian shoes. His perfectly combed, yet thinning, hair, his clean-shaven face, his ridiculous briefcase—seriously, who still carries a briefcase? He is a nerd, and I didn't even realize it. But now, he is gone, and I am free to redefine myself.

Yes, that's what I'll do. Make a change. The change has to start within me. Am I brave enough to go through with it? I have to try. If nothing else, I can fake it until I make it. I have survived far worse than Joe dumping me. I survived my past, and I will survive this.

It is time for a brand-new Jessica.

A Jessica who tries new things. And I know what that new thing will be. The only question that remains is, am I brave enough to go through with it?

CHAPTER SIX

Eager for my transformation, I waste no time. The next day, after work, I debut the new Jessica. With a dash of crimson on my lips, I look younger, more alive. Tonight, I am going to do something different. Something new. Really put myself out there, become someone else. My current person is a *drag*.

I can do it, I assure myself.

When Joe first ended things, one of my girlfriends, Kayci, offered to take me out to a bar—to dust off my cobwebs and meet a man. Not a Mr. Right, but a Mr. Right Now. I've never had a one-night stand, but apparently it's a cure for a broken heart. I am skeptical that is true, but Kayci insists it will empower me. But considering Kayci just popped out kid number two, I am on my own again. A single singleton. It will be a true test to see if I can really go to a bar alone and pick up a man.

Thinking back, I believe Wanda has been right. I need to do something different, something to snap me out of my funk. I've been happy before and I can be happy again. This is the shock to my system that I need.

With a breath, I run my fingers through my shoulder-length brown hair. I am ready to get out there. Ready to be different.

No longer will I let a man decide my happiness. I am going to take charge.

Inside a local hotel, known for catering to a more business clientele, I walk out of the restroom and over to the bar. I have worn high heels for the occasion—two-inch pumps. My pencil skirt and button-down blouse are the best "going out" clothes I can come up with on short notice, but a few undone buttons showing a hint of skin will have to do the trick. I tell myself, "I will not be afraid of talking to a man. I will not be worried they might not like me." It used to feel like the worst thing that could ever happen, but not tonight. *I am determined.*

After surveying the scene, I sit on the first available barstool. Two men are on the other side, with only one stool between us. They look to be in their early forties. One of them wears a wedding band, and the other looks unattached and is mildly attractive. Never have I been the aggressor, but I know I have to start a conversation to get the ball rolling. What will I say?

I've never gone to a bar trying to meet anyone—previous relationships were usually people I'd met through friends or at a party. Am I completely out of my depth? *No. I can do this.* They are just humans, after all. What is the worst that could happen?

The men don't talk to me or offer a friendly smile. They certainly don't offer me a drink. All proof I have to put my big girl undies on and make a move.

Soon, the bartender appears in front of me, his dark hair pulled back into a ponytail. He has tan skin and is strikingly handsome. He looks young, maybe in his early twenties, but maybe that isn't a bad thing. His warm smile catches me off guard.

"What can I get you?" he asks.

I am about to order my typical chardonnay, but that is the old me. The new me needs something different. "Tequila," I say with a boldness I don't quite feel yet.

He raises an eyebrow. "Tequila, huh? What kind? We have a menu, or I can give you a recommendation if you'd like."

I vaguely remember some coworkers talking about a tequila tasting they had gone to. I hadn't been part of the conversation, but I'd overheard them. Apparently, Clase Azul is a favorite. I take a breath. "Do you have Clase Azul?"

"Yes, I do," he says, his smile widening. "Would you like a lime and salt on the rim?"

"Just lime," I say. Salt will make me bloat, and I don't need to get any bigger. As it is, I've gained at least ten pounds since Joe dumped me.

"Coming right up." The bartender turns around, reaching up to the top shelf for the blue and white tequila bottle. I watch his back, his arms—he is fit. No ring on his finger.

He pulls down the bottle and sets a shot glass on the counter. It isn't one of those tiny, cheap ones. This glass is classy. It can hold at least four ounces. Like a mini rocks glass. He does the pour, grabs a lime from the bin, and sticks it on top of the glass. He sets it down on a napkin in front of me. "Enjoy."

I smile, for real. "Oh, I will."

I pick up the drink and glance over at the older men, who are now eyeing me—a single woman at the bar, ordering tequila. *That's right. I'm independent and in charge of my life.* Or does it read more like a sad, lonely woman taking shots by herself? *No, Jessica, don't think that way. You're a strong, confident woman. Fake it till you make it.*

I have read somewhere that confidence is sexy, and I know I can be confident and sexy. If I really try. I tip my head at them, acknowledging their presence, and take a sip of the tequila, bracing myself for the harsh taste I remember from college.

Slowly, the liquid burns a path down my throat, but there is a hint of vanilla. It isn't bad. I can get used to this. The men still don't talk to me. Maybe I am too confident for them. Maybe they want someone they can control, someone spineless. If they met me a week ago, they might have had just that.

But that woman is gone for good.

The two men, with their Dockers and button-down shirts, toss some cash on the bar, wave at the bartender, and leave.

Perhaps they're in a hurry. No big loss, I suppose. They remind me too much of Joe, anyway. I don't want another Joe.

The bartender returns. "How is it?"

"It's great, actually. I've never had it before, but a friend recommended it."

"Your friend has good taste."

"I think so."

"Can I get you any food, or just the drink for tonight?" he asks, a few buttons of his shirt undone, exposing a hint of his dark chest hair.

I consider it for a moment, staring at him. "I'll take a menu, please."

"Sure thing." He casually grabs a menu and sets it in front of me.

I haven't eaten, which, in hindsight, I should have. But if it means sitting there longer, scoping out the bartender, then so be it. I wonder if the hotel has rooms available. Should I have gotten one already? What if I take a man back to my room, and he turns out to be a crazy person? What if he is a serial killer? Ignoring the thoughts that plagued me during my younger years, preventing any random hookups, I move on with the plan.

The bartender is looking yummier and yummier each time I eye him. I definitely need a room for the night, at least for an hour or two. It would make more sense to have one ready, just in case. I can always tell the sexy bartender I am from out of town and, if he is interested, invite him to join me after his shift. If he isn't off for a few hours, I can go up to the room, freshen up, and be ready for when he is.

He stands near as I study the menu options. I don't want anything that will make me retain water or anything that will make me look unappealing while I eat it. I need to be sexy.

"I'll have the hummus and veggies."

"Excellent choice," he says with that flirty grin.

He turns his attention to other customers, and I quickly finish my tequila. Feeling a rush of nerves and excitement, I hurry over to the reservations desk.

"Can I help you?" the receptionist asks.

"I'd like a room for the night."

"Do you have a reservation?"

"No."

"No problem. Looks like we have plenty of availability." We exchange details and pleasantries, and the transaction is over quickly. I tuck the key card into my clutch and head back to the bar.

By the time I return, my plate of carrot sticks, cucumber slices, pita bread, and hummus is already waiting for me. I sit down and place a napkin on my lap. The bartender returns, his eyes sparkling. "Can I get you anything else?"

"Another tequila, please," I say. Still feeling antsy, I figure a little liquid courage might help.

I pick up a carrot, chewing each bite while watching him, wondering if he's catching on to my interest in him. My eyes follow his every move, studying his body, hoping to see more. Halfway through my plate of veggies, he comes back over.

"Pretty good, huh?"

"It's delicious."

"Anything else I can get you? Oh, right, your tequila? Give me one sec." He turns to grab the bottle before pouring my drink.

I cock my head and study him as he works, our eyes meeting in the mirror behind the bar. He knows I am watching him. He gives me a playful wink, and my heart races. This is really going to happen. *I am going to do this.*

Am I really about to invite a man up to my hotel room? My heart is pounding. What is the worst that could happen? If he isn't interested, he'll simply say no. I'll end up spending the night alone, but at least I'll have tried.

With another tequila in front of me, I know I have to keep drinking until I find the courage to ask for what I really want—him. I have never been with a stranger before. I have always needed to date someone for a while, too cautious and too afraid of the risks. My college friends bragged about their wild one-night stands, but I was never brave enough.

But here, in this hotel bar, it feels different. Surely, if he tries anything terrible, someone will hear, and there are surveillance cameras everywhere. Besides, he seems like a decent guy. I take a sip, then another, and then another.

"So," I say. "What's your name?"

"I'm Daniel," he says. "And you are?"

"Penelope," I say, looking coy. "Nice to meet you." I take another sip, draining my second shot. Feeling a surge of that liquid courage, I ask, "What time do you get off?"

He licks his lips. "I get off at ten."

It is only 8:30. I take a breath and say, "I'm staying in the hotel. Maybe you'd like to come up after your shift... for a nightcap?"

He grins, his teeth perfectly white. Is he amused by the idea of a slightly older woman picking him up? Or is he intrigued? I am doing something brave, something daring—but possibly something very stupid.

Oh geez. I hadn't even thought about condoms. Well, he doesn't get off until ten, so I have time to go to the store in the hotel lobby. I really haven't thought this all the way through. But it will be okay. I'll get the condoms, and everything will be fine.

I give him my room number, and he flashes me another smile. "I'll see you later," he says with a wink, and sets down the leather folio with my check inside.

As he walks over to help other customers, I can't help but wonder how many women have picked him up like this. How many has he been with? Is he careful? Does he have any diseases?

After leaving him a hefty tip, I shake off my nerves and head toward the hotel gift shop. I buy the condoms, tucking the small box discreetly into my purse. Adrenaline soars through me as I head back to my room.

Inside, a bit of panic and insecurity flares up. Will he laugh at my naked body? Think I am too pudgy once I pop out of my Spanx? I haven't been with a man besides Joe in over a decade. Has sex changed since then? I pace nervously, wondering if I am really going to go through with this. Have I made the right decision? I haven't brought a change of clothes or anything sexy to wear. But then, I reassure myself, my bra and underwear are lacy and they match, and that is sexy enough, right?

A knock on the door sounds, and my heart races. *It's go time.*

CHAPTER SEVEN

Light filters in through the thin hotel room curtains, casting pale streams across the bed. My eyes flutter open, and I immediately raise a hand to shield them from the brightness. Squinting, I turn to glance at the clock on the nightstand.

Panic jolts through me. It's almost 9:00 AM. I shoot up to a sitting position, heart pounding. I'm supposed to be at work by nine. How did I oversleep? How did I sleep through the relentless morning light seeping in through the curtains?

I look to my left, then to my right. I'm alone. The hotel room is silent, empty. There are no sounds of running water from the bathroom, no clinking from the sink or the thud of footsteps. There is no sign of the man I shared the bed with last night. No man asking what I'm making for breakfast or if I'm going grocery shopping that day. *I like it.*

As I process that, memories of the night before flicker back to me. Images of tequila shots, a carefree rush, and Daniel's alluring grin replay in my mind. He is sexy, young, and exudes a raw, magnetic energy. Our encounter was spontaneous, thrilling, and empowering in a way I didn't expect. Kayci was one hundred percent right. I think to myself, *Daniel, you're great. I'll never forget you. But let's not keep in touch.*

I pull the covers up to my chest and exhale, a small smile tugging at my lips. For years, I lived cautiously, refusing to go home with strangers out of fear they'd turn out to be murderers. I conjured countless nightmare scenarios—being chopped to pieces and left in a field somewhere. How ridiculous was I? How many serial killers even exist these days, anyway?

I glance back at the clock and know I need to make a choice. Go to work, or embrace this rare, untamed moment in my life. No one has ever told me how liberating sex could be or explained the surge of power that comes with being desired, purely and passionately. No strings attached. My cheeks flush. I don't think I've ever felt so irresistible, so wanted by anyone.

Maybe that was the allure of the night. I didn't know him, but perhaps that is what makes it so intoxicating. I feel like a different person. The version of me that worries about consequences, who always plays life on the safe side, is gone.

The room has grown brighter. I look around, trying to locate my phone, and spot it lying on the floor, half-hidden by my hastily discarded skirt. Pulling back the covers, I realize I'm wearing nothing. I can't even remember the last time I fell asleep completely naked.

I pad across the room, the carpet quiet against my bare feet, and pick up my phone.

Opening the email app, I quickly compose a message to my boss. "Caught something," I tap. "Could be the flu, or maybe even COVID. Don't want to risk it. I'll be out today." I chuckle aloud as I hit send.

What does it matter, anyway, if I take a day to myself? Today, I am free to do whatever I want. And for once, I am going to savor every second.

So this is what control feels like—power over my life. I want to march in a parade, scream from the rooftops, "Women, open your eyes! Take control! You're in charge!" Yes, this is the new me. No more Jessica. I am *Jess*, now, and I love it.

After I shoot off the email, I take a moment to glance around the hotel room. My outfit from the night before lays scattered around—my skirt on the floor, high heels tossed near the foot of the bed. My Spanx have to be somewhere, probably hiding in a corner or under the covers. I spot my blouse crumpled near the entrance to the bathroom.

An overnight bag with a change of clothes would have been nice, but come to think of it, I don't want anything from my old life. I'm craving something new, something that screams "Jess" instead of the outdated, boring Jessica.

I'll have to go shopping. Until then, I'll shower and put on my clothes from the previous night. Adding to my set of firsts, I'll have my first walk of shame. *Screw that.* There is no shame in what I did. I'll walk out, head held high in my skirt, wrinkled blouse, and pumps like I am a *frickin' queen*.

Today, I'll pamper myself. Get my nails done, perhaps some bold highlights for my hair—maybe even blue or pink tips. I can't remember when I felt more free than I do right now.

But as my excitement builds, my mind drifts back to the box in my apartment. That sad, dusty apartment from my old life. The box with my New Soundz jacket and scrapbook—relics of a time when I felt free and full of joy—before I became a woman constantly running as fast as I can, trying to reach an impossible destination, trying to measure up and never feeling good enough. Trying to be anyone but my mother and my circumstances. It had been twenty years since I felt this level of excitement. *How brutally sad.*

It feels like I have finally awakened from a bad dream. I have been living in slow motion, but no longer. Now awake, I'm ending the nightmare. I am ready to leave everything behind—

my wardrobe, my expectations, and the suffocating sense of duty. Maybe I'll even indulge in a proper breakfast, with carbs and everything. No more restricting myself all day only to end up ordering DoorDash while zoning out in front of the TV at night and then hating myself for it. That was post-divorce Jessica. The Jessica of yesterday.

From now on, I'm going to do what makes me feel good. I'm going to be the person I always wanted to be. I stand tall, adopting a power pose, and imagine the incredible future ahead.

My phone pings, shattering the moment. With a sigh, I pick it up. It is an email from my boss.

"Sorry you're not feeling well, Jessica," it says. "Will you be working from home? We really need to meet that Monday deadline. Thanks."

I exhale sharply, my jaw tightening. "Screw that," I mutter, my voice echoing through the empty room. I want to throw my phone across the room. Instead, I toss it onto the bed with a scowl. Perhaps not *just* a day off. It occurs to me that maybe I'll never go back.

CHAPTER EIGHT

BACK INSIDE MY pathetic little apartment, I kick off my heels, and they fly across my cramped living room. One of them hits the stack of boxes that Joe brought over three days ago. I deliberately ignore them and make my way into my tiny bedroom.

I pull on a pair of jeans, ones I bought somewhat recently after outgrowing my old pairs. They fit snugly, and I slip on a fresh bra, one with no itchy lace to annoy me while I shop until I drop.

Once I'm decked out in new Jess clothes, I'll go out for a night on the town. Or a local bar to pick up another conquest.

It's funny, realizing how much power women really have in the bedroom. At least, that's how it felt last night. I told him everything I ever wanted. I have never been that honest before, always too inhibited to share my desires. But last night, I spoke up, and he did exactly what I asked, eagerly and without hesitation. It was exhilarating, and I'm definitely looking forward to more encounters like that. But first—new clothes, for the new me.

I slip on a simple V-neck T-shirt and turn toward my closet. Blazers, floral blouses, sensible shoes for work—it's a sea of brown and beige. Too much brown. My life has been devoid of vivid color for too long. As I think about my shopping trip, I decide I will buy color. No more muted tones, no more boring shades of beige. After the chaos of my childhood, I craved stability and simplicity, but my life has become dull, washed out, and suffocated by neutral hues. *An overcorrection.*

I swallow back a flood of memories from when I was a little girl. Things I keep buried, things I've never told anyone, not even my therapist. It won't help to talk about them. Those memories don't matter anymore, I tell myself, and I walk out of my closet, suddenly uninterested in anything it offers.

In the kitchen, I grab a coffee pod from the basket and load it into the mundane little machine on the counter. I deserve freshly brewed coffee; the kind made from rich, fragrant grounds. Not something squeezed out of a piece of plastic, as if I can't spare five minutes to enjoy the real thing. That's it—my whole life has been a series of little sacrifices like that. I beat myself up so many times, for eating too much and not exercising enough or not being enough—and for what? Where has it gotten me?

Alone. At thirty-five, I am right back where I started. Alone as a child with parents too wrapped up in their own lives to pay attention to me. Heartbroken by a husband who doesn't want to stick around. Friends who no longer can relate to me. Sacrificing my true happiness has earned me nothing. No happy ending, no fulfilling life—just more loneliness.

The machine beeps, signaling that my coffee is ready. I open the fridge, pull out some oat milk, and pour it into my cup. My eyes drift back to the boxes in the living room. One of them holds the scrapbook Rochelle and I put together when we were kids. She made one just like it. The thought makes my heart heavy.

I set my coffee down and walk over to the boxes. There has

to be more inside than just the jacket and the scrapbook. I rifle through the contents, and sure enough, there is a stack of letters from Rochelle. A tingling sensation creeps down my arm, and a wave of memories and emotions rises up.

I grab the stack of letters and my coffee, sinking onto the couch. I glance at the address on the first envelope. It's the address of the house we lived in after we moved away from Rochelle. After two precious years seeing her nearly every day, my mom and her latest boyfriend split up, and Mom insisted we had to move again. We moved far away from the community I loved, the friends who made life bearable, and the sense of belonging I so desperately craved.

I hold my breath and open the first letter. "Hey Jess," it begins, and I remember she used to call me Jess. Not Jessica. "How's your new school? Anybody cute? Anybody who loves The New Soundz just like us?"

I keep reading, each word pulling me back to that time. Rochelle's letters are full of updates, little stories about her life as a tenth grader—all stories that don't include me. She still had other friends, parents who cared about what she did, and a home that felt stable. Meanwhile, I was alone, struggling to find my place in a new school where I didn't connect with anyone.

My days that used to be filled with Rochelle and our little girl group—all connected by our shared obsession for the New Soundz—were over in what felt like a flash. Ripped from that life, I wasn't sure I'd survive. But Rochelle and I insisted it couldn't be over. Neither of us were willing to let go simply because fifty miles lay between us.

We sent handwritten letters because I didn't have a computer at home or a cell phone. There was no money for that. We wrote to each other constantly, pouring our hearts out onto paper, and we talked on the phone when we could. Rochelle's mom, Tina, picked me up or drove Rochelle out to see me every few months. I didn't know what I would have done without Rochelle and Tina.

A tear rolls down my cheek as I realize how much I miss her and that vivid world we created together. It was a bubble of technicolor happiness, where everything was exciting, interesting, and dramatic. We screamed with glee every time our favorite song came on the radio, even though we played that CD a thousand times.

But my family ruined that, too. They couldn't stop for five minutes to think about what tearing me away from my life would do to me. Maybe they did think about it and just didn't care.

I used to think, *At least I have my letters from Rochelle.* Until they stopped. *Abruptly. Violently.*

Shoving the first one back in its envelope, I feel a deep sadness in my heart for all I have lost. Not only Rochelle but a simpler, happier time. When we lived in the moment and accepted all the joy that came our way. When we didn't worry about a five-year plan or appearances or counting calories. We lived on pizza, candy, ice cream, and endless cans of soda. The idea of drinking soda now makes me laugh. When was the last time I had a soda?

Why do all the good things have to end?

My phone buzzes, snapping me out of my memories. I glance at the screen. It is a second email from my boss, and I still haven't replied to the first one. With a sigh, I begin typing a response. "I have a raging headache," I write. "I'm laying down, trying to rest. Not sure I'll be able to work on the project. Sorry."

I pause, re-read my message, and then delete the word "sorry." Why should I apologize for being sick? I tap, "Hopefully, I'll get better soon," and hit send. Rolling my eyes, I throw the phone across the room. It hits the wall with a thud. Screw that job. It certainly doesn't bring me any joy.

After I wipe the tears off my face, I remind myself that I have control over my happiness now. People like my boss, who think I should work even when I am supposedly sick, have no power over me. She doesn't know that I'm not *actually* sick. But even if I was, I shouldn't have to work. I deserve to rest and I deserve to take care of myself.

No one has ever taken care of me—not as a child, not as an adult, not in the workplace. No one but me to do the job. I sip my coffee, a sense of resolve building within me. It's time to do things for myself, on my own terms. The phone buzzes across the room, but I don't care who is calling. I grab my purse, pick up the phone without checking the notification, and exit my sad apartment. It's time for me to become someone new.

CHAPTER NINE

THE SOUND OF A PHONE RINGS, and I jerk awake. Sweat drips down my temples and I gasp for air. After a few deep breaths, I shake my head as I break down into a mess of tears. I wail into the empty hotel room, "Why?" as I tear off my comforter. "Why?" I ask again as I kneel down onto the ground and bang my fists on the mattress.

My phone rings again.

Sobbing, I mumble, "I don't want to remember. I don't. I can't do it again." It has been years since I had *the nightmare*. The one that breaks my heart every time. The one where she leaves me all alone.

My mind flashes back to that day.

I screamed, "No!" and threw my CDs at the wall, one at a time, scratching the paint and cracking the discs. "I hate you! I hate all of you!"

My mother tried to get me to calm down, one of the few times I can remember her trying to embrace me in a hug, but I pushed her away. She was the last person I wanted to be near. There was no calming me.

I didn't get out of bed or go to school for a week. It was a dark week filled with even darker thoughts—the first time I considered that this world didn't have anything left for me.

My phone buzzes again, knocking me back to the present.

Taking in my surroundings, I glance around the luxurious hotel room I've called home for the last two days. Days I spent shopping, dining, and indulging in spa treatments. In control and filling up on joy. As if I can escape the emptiness inside me. Can I really start over? Or am I having some kind of mental breakdown?

Maybe the call is from work checking in to see if I am still "terribly ill" and unable to come in? Am I hasty in thinking I can leave it all behind and become someone new? Have I made a terrible mistake? Do I need to get myself together and return to my old life? The old Jessica?

No. I can't.

I climb off the floor and walk over to the desk, where my phone lies charging next to the hotel book. With a shaking hand, I pick it up and see it isn't from my boss. It is a text from Joe. Anger flares as I stare at the screen. Why is he texting me?

I open the message.

> Where are you? Can you call me?

Call him? Why on earth would I call him? But curiosity gets the better of me. Maybe he has found more of my boxes. *The boxes.* That is why the nightmares and the pit in my stomach have returned. The New Soundz and Rochelle, two of my biggest loves and two of my greatest heartbreaks. I shuffle into the grand bathroom and wash my face and drink a glass of water. *Get it together, Jess. You got this. It was only a nightmare. You are a strong and confident woman. Push down the darkness, go toward the light.*

I return to my phone and call Joe. He answers on the second ring.

"Where have you been?"

Hello to you too, jerk. "What do you mean?"

"We've been trying to deliver the final divorce papers to you, but you haven't been home or at work. Is everything okay?" His words come out in a rush, like he can't wait to be rid of this last tether between us.

I close my eyes, my hand curling into a fist. So that's why he's so desperate to reach me. He just can't stand to wait another day for my signature on those divorce papers, can't wait to move on and marry his new girl. Probably wants to pop out a bunch more babies so little Joey has siblings.

I take a deep breath and force myself to stay in control. "I've been away. Is it urgent?"

"You sound strange," he says, and I can hear the irritation under the surface. "Look, I just really want this to be done with."

"I'm sure you do, *Joe*." My voice drips with sarcasm.

"What is that supposed to mean?"

He hasn't met the new Jess yet—the one who doesn't fall for his faux sincerity. The one who doesn't buy into his condescending tone, his fake apologies. "Oh, I'm so sorry about all of this. I never meant to hurt you. I'm not a bad guy." Yeah, right. Or maybe he is sincere, considering he'd likely never even thought about me enough to do it on purpose.

"Just that you've always only cared about yourself, Joe," I say coldly. "I'm busy, and I'll get to the papers when I can. I'll let you know when I'm back in town."

There is a beat of silence.

"Are you okay?"

"Joe, I've never been better. Thanks for finally asking if I'm okay," I say. "Have a nice life." And with that, I hang up, tossing the phone onto the bed. I mutter, "Screw him and everyone else who thinks they can walk all over me." Blood boiling, I say, "They can't control me anymore!"

I shake my head, and then I freeze. A grin slowly spreads across my face. Darkness shoved down, I hurry over to the phone, pick it up, and pull up one of my playlists. I hit play on "Girl, I Love You," by the New Soundz, and the opening chords fill the room. As the music swells, I dance toward the closet, singing along with abandon.

"I love you," I belt out, twirling in front of the mirror. "And I always will!" I sing to my new clothes, the ones I spent hours picking out, feeling the beat of the music throughout my body.

As I twirl around, I know tonight is going to be special because new Jess is going out.

CHAPTER TEN

Perched on the barstool, wearing my new red jumpsuit, I sit poised and confident. As I find myself in the position for a second time, I imagine how I'll approach my next conquest. I can already picture how effortless it will become after a few tries—how natural it'll feel. The anticipation vibrates under my skin, and everything feels right.

The bartender approaches. He is an older man, probably around sixty, with thinning hair, faded tattoos on his forearm, and a warm, friendly smile. "Hi, I'm Jordan. What can I get you tonight? Just a drink, or having dinner too?"

"I'm having both," I say, returning a scarlet smile.

"All right, let me grab you a menu," he says and walks off.

I watch him for a moment. He seems kind, but he won't be lover number two. Should I keep a list? It isn't a bad idea—a diary or a notebook to keep track of my lovers. Who knows, maybe one day I'll write a memoir. I'll call this my liberation era. I am liberating myself from a world that has held me with metaphorical chains. Broken free, I can find my true self.

Jordan returns with the menu, interrupting my thoughts. I thank him before flipping through the cocktail options. I consider ordering tequila again, but this is a classy place. Maybe I should order a white wine. It will make me seem a little less intimidating, a little more refined. Plus, sipping a glass of wine gives me more time to savor the atmosphere while waiting for the right man to approach.

Glancing up at him, I say, "I'll have the chardonnay."

"Great, I'll get that right out for you."

Jordan would likely be easy to get, but he isn't my type anymore. I've been married to a man fifteen years my senior and know that, for a fun romp, I'd be better off with a younger, more virile man. Plus, I like them young, like Daniel—lover number one. He was thrilling and spontaneous, and he made me feel powerful.

Jordan returns with the glass of chardonnay and sets it in front of me. "Are you ready to order food?"

"Yes, I'll have the gnocchi, and I'll start with the beet salad."

"Great, I'll get those right out for you."

I thank him, feeling a rush of satisfaction. Everything about tonight feels perfect, the ugliness of the morning gone and buried deep. Confidence restored.

I glance down at my outfit. The jumpsuit I've chosen hugs all the right places, showing off my assets in a way that feels sophisticated, not over the top. My hair is freshly styled from earlier today—a trim with new highlights: blonde with subtle red streaks. *Dangerous.* I giggle quietly to myself, feeling bold.

I sip my wine, wondering how long I'll have to wait for the perfect guy to come along. It's the kind of place that attracts after-work professionals, visiting businessmen, and maybe a few locals. Perhaps a tech billionaire will walk in, I think, amused. The possibilities seem endless. Who will be next?

I catch his scent before I see him—sandalwood, warm and inviting. I turn to my right, and there he is: a man in his early thirties, wearing a crisp white button-down shirt and dark denim jeans. His hair is golden and his eyes bright-blue. He catches my gaze and gives me a charming smile.

"Good evening," he says.

"Good evening."

"How's your night going?"

"It's pretty great so far. You?"

"It's great *now*." He flashes another smile, and a thrill runs through me. He is here for the same reason I am. I plan to have dinner, but as I look at him, I think he could be my dessert.

The bartender returns, setting my salad down in front of me. "Enjoy," he says, giving a knowing look to my new friend, as if he recognizes him. With a slight nod, Jordan moves on to help other patrons.

I pick up my fork, spear a dark red beet from my salad, and pop it into my mouth, eyeing the stranger beside me.

"Dining alone?" he asks.

"Yes," I say, "and you?"

"Same. Mind if I join you? I could use a few bites."

"As you wish," I say with a small, inviting smile.

He lifts a hand to get the bartender's attention. "Hey Jordan, can I get a burger and fries?"

"You got it."

I study him, intrigued. "Come here often?"

"I work nearby and tend to stop by after work when I don't feel like going home and rummaging through my near-empty fridge."

"So, what do you do…?" I pause, giving him an opportunity to fill in the blank space I leave for his name.

"I'm Sam," he says, offering a firm handshake. "And I'm in finance."

Sam in finance. He is well-built, his presence strong. Perhaps that is enough, I think, already imagining the evening ahead. "And you?" he asks.

"Jess," I say smoothly.

"Jess," he repeats, savoring the sound of my name. "Are you from out of town?"

"I am," I say. "Just here on vacation."

He glances down at my hand and then says, "It's very nice to meet you, Jess. Thank you for letting me join you. I'd say it's my lucky night."

"Of course," I say. Hopefully, there won't be too much conversation. I am not looking for attachment, and I don't think he is either. We are both here for something simple and satisfying.

I finish my salad while he launches into a ramble about the stock market, punctuating his speech with statistics I barely register. As my gnocchi and his burger arrive, I realize I've already drained my glass of wine and gesture for another.

"Jess, what do you do when you're not on vacation?" he says in between bites.

I almost tell him the truth—that I am a computer programmer. But then I decide that maybe this encounter calls for a different persona altogether. The last man got a fake name; maybe this one deserves a fake profession. "I'm a social media manager," I say, improvising.

"Oh? Which industry?"

"Beauty," I add, keeping the details vague.

"Interesting. Very interesting." He leans back. "How long are you in town?"

Best to keep things simple. "Just tonight," I say. "Then I head home."

He smiles knowingly. "Good to know."

I mirror his grin, and a thrill shoots through me. There is a language to these things: the subtle dance of one-night encounters. A wink, a smile—both parties understand with no need to say it outright.

We chat about the weather, travel, and mundane topics until Sam finishes his dinner and excuses himself to use the restroom.

Moments later, Jordan the bartender returns. "How's everything tasting?"

"It's great, thanks."

Jordan hesitates, then lowers his voice. "Be careful with that guy. His intentions aren't always noble."

I raise an eyebrow. "No?"

"No, just... be safe," he says, looking genuinely concerned.

I smile and wave him off. "Don't worry. I'm a big girl. I can take care of myself."

"Okay, I just thought I'd let you know," he says, giving me a slight nod before walking away.

Is Jordan, the bartender, just another man thinking I need protection? A little girl in a man's world? I don't need anyone to look out for me and am more than capable of taking care of myself.

Sam returns shortly after.

"Did you enjoy your dinner?"

"It was great," I say, pushing my empty plate aside. "Yours?"

"Satisfying. Now, I'm quite keen for a bit of dessert." He leans in with a playful glint in his eye. "Do you have room for dessert?"

I tilt my head, matching his energy. "I'd love dessert, but not anything that is on the restaurant's menu."

He gives me a lopsided grin. "Do you have a room upstairs?"

"I do." I raise my hand, signaling to Jordan. "Check, please."

CHAPTER ELEVEN

My body feels like it's filled with lead, every muscle weighted down with an aching heaviness. I can't move, can't even muster the strength to lift my head. What time is it? My hand feels unsteady as I reach up to touch my skull, which pulses with a relentless, blinding pain. Each beat of my heart echoes in my head, sending fresh waves of agony crashing through me. *How much did I drink last night?*

I force my eyes open, wincing as sunlight streams through the thin curtains. Harsh, golden light fills the room, and I squint against it, feeling the air press down on me. Everything feels too bright, too loud, and too overwhelming.

I scan the room, my heart thumping unevenly. He is gone. *Good.* Relief is fleeting, a shallow breath that does nothing to calm the dread building in my chest. I turn to the nightstand and squint at the glowing numbers on the clock: 5:07. That can't be right. It's light out, far too bright to be five in the morning. I reach for my phone, my fingers clumsy and uncoordinated, and check the time. It is indeed 5:07 in the *evening*. It is Saturday. I have slept through almost an entire day.

Panic twists in my gut as I lower the phone. Something is

wrong. I glance down at my wrists, and my breath catches in my throat. Bruises, dark and angry, circle my skin like cruel bracelets. What happened? A chill runs down my spine, and dread coils tighter. My mind races, but every thought feels sluggish, muffled by the fog in my head.

I slowly climb off the bed, each movement agonizing. My limbs feel disconnected, alien. I am not wearing any clothes. That part isn't a shock—I expect that, given last night's intentions but now everything feels wrong and terrifying.

I stumble to the bathroom, my feet dragging on the carpet. Upon flicking on the light, the fluorescent glare pierces my skull like a dagger. I wince, lowering my gaze, giving my eyes time to adjust. *How much did I drink?* Slowly, hesitantly, I lift my head and look in the mirror.

My reflection makes my blood run cold. Bruises mar my neck, dark marks shaped like fingers pressing into my skin. Red blotches cover my chest, my arms, and my cheek—an angry handprint stands out on my face. I raise a trembling hand, my fingertips brushing the throbbing skin at my temple. *How did this happen?* My head aches, my mind a swirling mess of confusion and fear.

Everything feels hazy, like I am swimming through a thick fog. I want to lie down, to close my eyes and shut out the pain, but a voice yells at me, "Don't sleep. Don't close your eyes." Panic surges, and for a moment, I can't remember why. Why shouldn't I?

Then, with a sudden, sickening clarity, it hits me. I might have a concussion and can't go back to sleep. I need to get to the hospital. The fear morphs into urgency, cutting through the haze. But moving feels like trying to hike a mountain after drinking an entire bottle of tequila.

Fragments of the night before return, each one hitting me like a physical blow. *Sam.* He comes up to my room. He has a flask and offers it to me and I accept happily. But then the room spins soon after. He presses me down onto the bed. His hands are at my neck. I tell him no, again and again. I want to be in control. That's why I am here, why I set out on this whole stupid adventure. But he doesn't listen.

His hands are on my throat, squeezing until I can't breathe. His voice echoes in my ears. "You'll like it, trust me." But I don't. I can't fight him. He slaps me, the force of it snapping my head to the side. I remember the way I struggle, the way my strength drains from me until I am nothing but a limp, broken thing beneath him.

Tears stream down my face, and my body trembles, each sob wracking through me. The memories are a crushing weight, but they aren't just from last night. Older, buried memories claw their way to the surface: pain, fear, helplessness, and guilt from times I tried so hard to forget.

The worst possible thoughts break through. Maybe I can't be new. Maybe I've been all wrong. Happiness is for other people, not for me.

This time I've been beaten. Maybe next time I'll be dead. A sinking feeling and the all-too-familiar question returns. Would I be better off dead? A final end to the tortured existence I live.

Something inside of me screams, *Go! Get help*. Where does that inner voice come from? Is it her guiding me? Has it always been her?

From the bathroom, I shuffle over to the dresser. My hands shake so hard I almost can't grip the handle. I pull out a pair of new jeans, the ones that hug every curve. Sliding them on is torture; every movement feels like fire. I have to grip the edge of the bed to keep from collapsing.

Focus, Jess. I throw on a simple shirt, slip into my flip-flops, and grab my coat and bag. Every step toward the door is a battle, but I force myself onward. That man can't control me. He doesn't get to ruin me. I won't let him. I am still here, still fighting. And I am not giving up. *I can be new. Can't I?*

Shuffling out of my hotel room, I make my way to the taxi stand. My body screams in pain, but my mind burns with determination. My loss of control is temporary. This man, this monster, won't take my power. Not now. *Not ever.*

CHAPTER TWELVE

The taxi ride to the hospital feels endless, and soon thoughts of my old life as the old Jessica—the one I tried to leave behind just a few days earlier—come crashing to my mind. The idea of going back to the old Jessica seems terrible.

And it hits me that perhaps time off is in order. Real time off. Not just a few days. I can easily afford to take a year or two off of work. I've always been so diligent with money, scrimping and saving, making smart investments all with the future in mind. For what? So I can eventually shrivel up and die alone, enjoying the best nursing care money can buy?

Maybe I'll quit my job and take time off to figure out what I want to do with the rest of my life. Do I really want to keep coding in a cubicle for the next thirty years? A "no" screams in my mind. The thought of sitting at a computer, writing strings of commands and fixing bugs, makes me want to hide out forever.

And the idea of going back to that dreary apartment is too much to bear. I can't, but that means I have to find a new place to live. *I need to live.* This ordeal with Sam shows me I can't take life for granted and I *don't* want to die. I need to be smarter.

Safer. But I can't go back to my old life. My old job. That awful divorce apartment.

I should email my boss right now, give my notice, and be done with it. No two weeks' courtesy, just "Hi, I don't work here anymore." I don't have any personal effects in my office anyway, not since Joe left me. A framed photo of us on our wedding day used to sit on my desk, but I chucked it. The memory of me smiling up at him wearing a gorgeous white gown and promising to love him forever makes me queasy. And his family. *Ick*.

They always acted so perfect and looked down on mine like we were some sort of circus act. Sure, my family isn't great. They aren't even polite or kind all the time, not even when in front of company. But they're still people, right? They care—in their own way. At least, I have to believe that they do. Not everyone knows how to love or express love in a healthy way.

My mother loves me. I'm sure of it. She just never really knew how to show it. Especially when I see how she interacts with her own mother. *I understand.* My grandmother doesn't know how to show love either. They call that generational trauma. No one to blame, right? Just a cycle that keeps going.

And my father? Wherever he is, I'm sure he cares... or maybe he doesn't. I haven't seen him since I was five years old. Memories are fuzzy, and sometimes I wonder if I passed him on the street, if I'd recognize him or if he'd recognize me. Mom says he's a no-good junkie. All I can do is believe her.

So yeah, when Joe ended things, I cleared out my desk at work. Everything there reminds me of him, and I can't stand it. I don't want constant reminders of what a fool I've been, of what I think I've lost. Why did I fall in love with him in the first place? Because he paid attention to me? Bought me flowers? Said he loved me? All the things I'd never had before. I fell for all of it—I was easy pickings. But with my new life as Jess, I can see that all

I really lost was a 230-pound, fifty-year-old weight named Joe. *I want a do-over.*

Upon arrival at the hospital, I thank the driver and slowly climb out of the cab. Entering through the automatic doors of the Emergency Room, the hospital fills my senses with antiseptic and cold, sterile air. The fluorescent lights sting my eyes, and I feel small, exposed. Is everyone staring at me? Do they know what happened to me? Do they know I trusted the wrong man? That I let myself get drugged and attacked? Once a fool, always a fool? The voice in my head returns. *No, Jess. No negative thoughts.*

At the check-in station, I explain to the nurse that I might have a head injury. The woman squints her eyes and frowns before handing me forms to fill out and tells me to take a seat. After that, a reassuring nod that I read loud and clear—pity. Another statistic.

As I fill in my information, I wonder how many women have been in my position. I know a few. Are they like me? All alone, just trying to fill the hole inside them? I squeeze my eyes shut and try to push away the thoughts. My only purpose for the visit is to make sure I don't have a serious brain injury.

My physical body will heal, but not without medical attention. After I fill out the papers, I stand up and amble to the desk and hand the clipboard back to the nurse. She says, "It won't be long."

Fighting tears, I nod and return to my seat. I'm not sure what I hate more—that I let it happen or that this man will get away with it. So many men get away with it. When does it end?

To my surprise, only a few minutes later, another nurse calls my name. I raise my hand and head toward a thirty-something woman in blue scrubs. She guides me to an examination room as I clutch onto my purse.

"Can you tell me why you came in today?"

It occurs to me to make up a story, one that makes me sound less like a victim, but I surprise myself and tell her every detail I can remember. The outpouring of truth surprises me and despite my sobs, I feel a little better after. That inner voice that picked me up before returns again and says, *You're doing great, Jess. You got this.*

"Do you want to report this to the police?"

I wrap my arms around myself. "No."

"Are you sure? He could do this to someone else and likely has before."

"But it would be he said, she said. I consented to the alcohol that I think had some drug in it. I couldn't fight him."

"If you didn't know it was drugged, even if you did, if you said 'no' or told him to stop at any point, you did *not* consent."

Flashbacks to watching Law & Order SVU enter my mind. The broken woman on the witness stand. The man denying it all, saying she told him she likes it rough. I don't want to be her. Shaking my head, I say, "I don't want to."

"Okay," the nurse says, not pushing. "Do you consent to a sexual assault exam? It could be important later, even if you don't want to press charges now."

I swallow, my throat dry. Every instinct screams at me to say yes, to preserve some kind of evidence. But the thought of being poked and prodded, examined and questioned, makes my stomach twist. "No."

"How about checking for STDs?"

I need to know if he's given me a sexually transmitted disease. I've never had one before. Feeling more in control, I say, "Yes, let's check."

The nurse nods, her expression understanding, though there is a flicker of concern. "All right. I'll take your vitals, and then the doctor will come in and perform an exam and treat your injuries," the nurse says gently. "Is that okay?"

I nod again, eyes closed, as the nurse slips the cuff on my forearm to check my blood pressure. My body aches, but that is the least painful part of the experience. Deep buried memories are flooding my consciousness, and it is too much to bear.

A soft humming, clear and familiar, snaps me out of my memories. I open my eyes and glance at the nurse, who is now scribbling notes on a clipboard, humming a familiar tune.

"Is that..." My voice cracks. I swallow and try again. "Is that a New Soundz song?"

The nurse looks up. "Yeah, it is! 'Never Say Goodbye.'" She grins, her face lighting up. "Are you a fan?"

With the tiniest hint of a grin, I say, "I was. Some might say I was obsessed. I still know every word of every song."

"Me too!"

She reminds me of Rochelle and our first meeting. How we bonded instantly over the New Soundz. "It's funny. I was just going through an old box and found my New Soundz tour jacket and my old scrapbook."

"You had a tour jacket! I'm so *jealous*."

"It still fits." And with that realization, I feel a little lighter.

"Are you going to the concert?"

Concert? "I didn't know they were back together."

"They are! They're doing a residency in Las Vegas. I'm going to the first show in a few weeks. I'm *beyond* excited."

They're back together. I feel something shift inside me, a pull I can't quite explain. The New Soundz. The band I once adored with every fiber of my being. The music that lifted me out of some of the darkest times of my life. Hearing their name from a fellow Soundling, it feels like fate, like the universe is handing me a clue, a direction.

Earlier I questioned my choices, but in the end, I know I can't go back to my old life. I know I need to create a new life for myself and now, suddenly and with extreme clarity, I have a focus and a destination. *Las Vegas*.

"I'll have to see if they still have tickets available."

"I think they do. You should definitely go," she says. "You deserve it. Soundlings for life, right?"

With tears in my eyes, I nod. "Do you believe everything happens for a reason?"

"I do."

"Me too."

She pats me on the shoulder and says, "Dr. Hanford will be right in. She's great. You're in excellent hands. Take care." She pauses and sings, "And girl, I'll *always* love you."

With a tiny smile, I complete the lyrics, "And nothing could ever make us fall apart."

She gives me a wink and heads out of the exam room.

I leave the hospital with discharge papers and instructions I barely glance at. The doctor explained she didn't think I have a concussion, and the headache is likely from the drug he put in the flask. There isn't any sign of an STD, but they'll call me with the lab results. I'll be in pain for a little while but then should be fine. Overall, it's good news.

They wheel me outside into the chilly San Francisco air. And as I order a rideshare, I feel a shift in my universe. A purpose. Something I *must* do.

The rideshare arrives, and I climb inside.

On the drive to my hotel, I try not to think about the pain that pulses with every breath. Instead, I shift my focus to what I *need* to do.

As soon as I reach my room, I scan the Internet to learn everything I can about the New Soundz residency in Las Vegas. Because everything in me knows exactly where I need to be and exactly what I have to do. Not just for me but for Rochelle too. *I got you, girl*.

CHAPTER THIRTEEN

Four days later, armed with a plan and renewed confidence, I march into the apartment manager's office and hand her my thirty-day notice.

"May I ask why you're moving out so soon?"

After a week in my posh hotel, I know I have stuff to do and need to tie up a few things before I embark on my quest. "My year lease is coming up for renewal, and I have decided to try a new city."

"We're sad to see you go, but we wish you luck in the future."

"Thank you so much."

I leave the management office and head back to my apartment. Relief washes over me at the thought of finally leaving. The building's dull, beige walls with brown trim have always felt oppressive, like living in a world made entirely of bland oatmeal hues. I am done with beige. Done with monotony.

Once inside my apartment, I finish taping up the one box from my old life that I am taking with me. Just one box. It holds my New Soundz jacket, my old scrapbook, letters from

Rochelle, and a few family photos. Everything else will be trashed or dropped off at a donation center. All items on my to-do list before I start, *really start*, my new life. On that list is a goodbye to two of my closest friends.

I have to break the news in a few hours over a pre-planned dinner. We don't see each other as much as we used to because we're all wrapped up in our own lives. I have been lost in despair and them with all the duties that come with being working mothers and wives.

A sharp knock on the door sounds. *Who is that?* I'm not expecting anyone.

I hurry over and peer through the peephole. *Joe*. Of course. He has been persistent lately—more so than he ever was when we were together. He desperately wants my signature for the divorce to be final. I should just give it to him. With bigger and better things on the horizon, I certainly don't want him in my life any more than he wants me.

When I open the door, there he stands. Joe, with his thinning, receding hairline and a face that has taken on a ruddy tone over the years. A reminder of how much he has changed since we first met. Or maybe he hasn't changed at all. I remember how, when we were married, he tried to hide those first signs of aging, fussing over his hair in the mirror or asking if I could see the gray coming in.

"Hi, Joe," I say, irritation in my voice.

He looks at me with an expression I've seen a thousand times before—impatient, exasperated, and yet somehow expectant, as if he thinks he can still command my attention. "Where have you been?"

I stare straight into his eyes, refusing to back down. "It's none of your business where I've been, Joe."

He frowns, his brows pulling together. "Look, I don't know what's going on with you, but I need you to sign these papers."

My stomach twists. He has always been so focused on what he needs, never once stopping to think about what I want. "Oh, what's the big hurry, Joe?" I ask, crossing my arms. "Got some big plans to make?"

"Yes," he snaps. "We've set a wedding date."

My jaw clenches. I shouldn't feel anything, but there is still a twinge of pain, even if buried beneath layers of anger and disappointment. "Oh, I see. So, you need me to sign these papers, huh?"

"Why are you being like this, Jessica?" His eyes search my face, and I can tell he is genuinely confused. Maybe he thought this would be easier. Maybe he thought I am still the same woman he left behind, the one who will do anything to keep the peace.

"It's just *Jess* now," I correct him sharply. That name, Jessica, sounds too soft, too forgiving. I'm not that person anymore.

"Where is all this hostility coming from? What's on your neck? What happened to your face? Have you been in an accident?"

His concern feels like too little, too late. "It's not your business and none of your concern," I snap. "Give me the stupid papers. I'll sign them so you and your new little family can go live happily ever after." The anger in my voice surprises even me. Where does that come from? Maybe it is the years of pent-up frustration finally clawing their way out. Jessica would bury it deep inside, but Jess speaks her mind.

Joe shakes his head and hands me the packet. I take a step back, gesturing for him to come in. He hesitates before crossing the threshold, and I feel a flicker of unease coming from him. But there is something about him being on my turf that makes me feel stronger, not weakened like before. I kind of like it.

I slide the papers out of the envelope, my eyes scanning the words that mark the end of our marriage. Seeing it in writing makes everything feel so final, even though I have long accepted that we are over. It is final, and there is no point in dwelling on the past. What's done is done. Two years of dating and eight years of marriage, a time I thought was happy and forever—gone. I feel a pang, not for him, but for the naïve version of myself who believed in forever.

"Do you have a pen?" I ask, my voice steady despite the emotions roiling inside me.

Joe nods and pulls one from his jacket pocket, handing it over. I sign near the yellow tabs, one after another, and hand the pen and papers back. He looks at me, and for a moment, I wonder if he feels anything at all. Regret? Sadness? Anything? But his face is unreadable.

"You can leave now," I say coldly. "Good luck to you and my replacement."

"It doesn't have to be like this, Jessica."

I take a steadying breath. He has always been good at making me doubt myself. "I said it's just *Jess* now."

He rolls his eyes, and there it is, that same condescending look he used to give me. "Okay, *Jess*. I don't see any reason we can't be friends, or at least amicable."

"Really? You can't think of *any* reason, Joe? Are we going to meet for coffee and catch up on each other's lives? Are you going to invite me to your love child's first birthday? Is that really going to happen?"

"Fine," he says. "Forget I said anything. Good luck." He walks out of my apartment, and I watch as he leaves.

I bite my lip, trying to expel any remaining sadness. The history we share is heavy, and the relief of his departure is bittersweet. How did I ever fall for him? I have made so many mistakes in my life. Is he one of them—or was he a necessary step in finding who I really am?

Ignoring any lingering feelings regarding that wretched man, I focus on the box. The box that represents both joy and devastation... and a wrong that needs to be righted. *Trust me Rochelle, that is exactly what I'm going to do.*

CHAPTER FOURTEEN

As I walk into the restaurant to meet the gals, I try to shove down the anger and frustration of signing my divorce papers and having to see Joe and instead focus on all the upcoming plans. I want a fun evening and to share my big news. Kayci and Sophie are the closest thing I have to family, other than my addict mother and sister. I hope they support me because I don't think I could bear to lose them too. New Jess still loves them.

Greeted by an enthusiastic young hostess, I request a table for three, since I am the first to arrive. The place is softly lit, with the hum of conversation filling the air. Seated at the table, I am lost in my thoughts about what the future will hold, but soon, Kayci and Sophie appear, waving as they make their way over. They wear matching sweater sets, jeans, and practical sneakers—classic mom uniforms. They look happy, content, and effortlessly coordinated.

"Hi, ladies!"

"Hi, Jessica," Sophie says as she sits down, giving me a once-over. Her eyes widen slightly. "What happened?"

The dark bruises on my neck, wrists, and face have faded

into an awful yellow tinge that looks ghoulish. My new make-up hasn't been able to cover it completely.

Kayci leans in, her mouth agape. "Yeah, my gosh."

I swallow hard, forcing a small laugh. Everyone assumes I've been in an accident. Might as well go along with it, at least for now. I don't want to bring down the mood. "Oh, you know how clumsy I am," I say with a self-deprecating grin. "Took a tumble down the stairs. My heel got caught in my pant cuff. So stupid, really."

Sophie's face softens with sympathy. "I'm so sorry. That sounds terrible."

"Yeah, it was no picnic, but overall, I'm fine." The truth is, I still feel stiff, and the ibuprofen I've been popping is the only thing keeping the aches at bay. But I survived. *I'm a survivor*.

Kayci says, "That's good to hear. And your hair looks fantastic! And is that a new dress? You look *amazing!*"

"It is! I indulged in a little self-care." I leave out the part about staying in a hotel for a week and taking time off work because of the "COVID." That is a lot to explain, and I don't think they'd understand.

A young male server with well-muscled arms approaches our table, a friendly smile on his face. "Good evening, ladies. Can I get you something to drink, or do you need a moment with the menu?"

"A moment, please," I say, speaking for the table.

"Okay, I'll give you a minute." He hurries off, and I note he is kind of cute. But my days of casually flirting or picking up lovers are on pause—at least until my body heals and I know I can remain in control of the situation. No more sips from unknown origins or falling for someone like Sam, a predator disguised as a normal human being.

I glance at the menu, silently debating whether I should have alcohol. Wine isn't ideal for my healing process, but at this point, what could it hurt? Sophie turns to me, her eyes lighting up. "Chardonnay?"

Kayci says, "I'll go with Chardonnay, too. I need it. What a day." She rolls her eyes dramatically.

"Make that three. Should we just get a bottle?"

"Oh yes, an entire bottle!" Kayci cheers, and Sophie joins in with a laugh, as if ordering a bottle of wine between the three of us is an act of rebellion. I envy them and their simple happiness. Their lives are full of kids, husbands, and white picket fences. Once, that was what I wanted, too. Now, it seems wrong for me—nothing like the adventure I am about to embark on.

After the server returns and takes our order for a bottle of wine and an appetizer, I turn to Sophie. "So, what's new?"

"Well," Sophie begins, "we spent all week looking at the kids' school options. Jonathan wants to put the kids in private school, but I'd rather keep them in public. It's been so complicated. I went to public school, and I turned out fine!"

Kayci nods in agreement. "I feel like public schools are perfectly good."

"Yeah," Sophie sighs. The conversation shifts to discussions about their children and their husbands, full of minor complaints but underpinned with love. They are happy. I can see it, even if they won't always admit it outright. But happiness is different for everyone, isn't it?

The three of us met back in college when we were young and idealistic. We shared a dorm room and took to each other pretty quickly. Nothing like what Rochelle and I had, but it's nice to have friends whose company I enjoy and have common interests with. Back then, we all dreamed of husbands and babies and careers. They got all three. I just had the two. And now none of those. But perhaps I am about to have something entirely better.

It is clear now that what makes them happy wouldn't make

me happy. And what makes me happy wouldn't work for them. Each individual's path to joy is unique. In my last days at the hotel, I thought a lot about the concept as I soaked in the jetted tub full of bubbles.

When there is a pause, I take a breath. "I have some big changes coming up."

"Oh?" Sophie's sculpted eyebrows lift with interest.

Just then, the server arrives with our bottle of wine. We pause our conversation as he pours us each a glass. The crisp chardonnay sparkles in the light, and I savor the first sip, feeling a sense of lightness. He leaves us alone to enjoy our drinks, and I turn back to my friends. "I'm going on an extended vacation."

"You are? Where are you going?"

"I'm going to Las Vegas. I'm not sure for how long—maybe a month or two or three."

"Why Las Vegas?" Sophie asks.

It's a good question. I've never shown any interest in Las Vegas before and have never been there. "The New Soundz have a residency there and I want to see all the shows. It's kind of like a divorce present to myself."

Sophie's eyes widen with concern. "Did you get the papers yet?"

"Just signed them an hour ago. Joe stopped by, and he was quite eager for me to sign, considering he and his child bride set a date."

Kayci lets out a gasp.

I shrug, feigning indifference. "Honestly, I really don't care. I'm done with him. And I'm done with my job. I'm going to quit that, too." A laugh bubbles up, and I take a sip of wine before lifting my glass. "Ha! Here's to new adventures." Not that I officially quit my job. I simply stopped responding to my boss's annoying emails.

After a slight hesitation, Kayci says, "You seem happy about it."

"I am."

Kayci says, "That's great."

Sophie says, "Cheers to that!"

I feel warmth radiate from their support. Why did I expect judgment? They've been nothing but kind. They are true friends.

"Any ideas of what you'll do after the trip?" Sophie asks.

"No, not really. I have plenty of savings," I say, "and I'm just going to play it by ear for now. I've given up my apartment, so I'm going to be a bit of a nomad for a while."

Another stunned pause by Kayci while Sophie says, "That sounds so exciting, Jessica. I'm jealous! When do you leave?"

"I'm excited! I leave in three days!" I say, a smile growing on my face. My flight and hotel are booked. All I have left to do is clear out my sad apartment and then I'll be good to go.

"You'll have to send us a postcard when you get there," Kayci adds with a laugh. "Do people still send postcards?"

"I don't know." I chuckle. "But I'll send pics."

"Yes! Oh my!" Sophie exclaims. "I can't wait to hear about everything you do while you're there. It sounds like you're going to have the time of your life."

I will have the time of my life, but I certainly won't tell them everything I am planning to do in Las Vegas. I think, *That's just between you and me, Rochelle.* It would only make Kayci and Sophie complicit and they don't need that in their lives. They have found their happiness, and now it's my turn. I am going to chase my destiny, and I know that the New Soundz residency will be a part of that—not only hearing the songs and seeing their faces and rejoining my community of fellow Soundlings, but finding closure, too. Based on all the research I've done on the New Soundz and their tour, I am confident I'll find exactly what I'm looking for. Rather, *who* I'm looking for. With a wicked grin, I think, *Rochelle, he'll never see me coming.*

CHAPTER FIFTEEN

THE FLIGHT to Las Vegas was short and on time, with no turbulence. The taxi was swift and before I know it, I'm checked in at the hotel. A perfect beginning to my adventure.

A bellhop carries my box as I wheel my suitcase up to the suite. I thank him as he places my box gently on the ground. Inside, I look at my new home. There is a small but functional kitchen, a cozy living room with a large-screen TV, a comfortable bedroom in the back, and a spacious bathroom with a luxurious soaking tub. This is a definite upgrade from the bland, cramped apartment I've left behind.

I walk over to the window and look out, my heart rate increasing. There it is—the Las Vegas Strip, sprawling with neon signs and energy. And right across the street, I can see the Dolby Live, where, in a few weeks, the New Soundz will play night after night. Just the sight of it sends a thrill through me. *I am so close.* My heart thumps with excitement, and I can't help but smile.

But then, a shadow of sadness creeps in. My body tenses, and I think about Rochelle. I wish she were here, that we were still thick as thieves, sharing Red Vines, watching music videos, and singing along to their songs, like we used to. Those days are long gone, a part of a life that feels so distant. I have a new purpose now, but those plans don't include Rochelle. Not really. I didn't want it to be this way, but it wasn't my choice.

I shake off the dark thoughts, physically shuddering to push them away. This is supposed to be a new beginning, and I am determined to take it head-on. "Take the bull by the horns," I mutter to myself, already feeling a spark of determination. My plan is to head out and explore the New Soundz' new home—the Park MGM. Maybe I'll get lucky and catch a glimpse of the stage or see the roadies setting up. The odds of catching the guys practicing are slim, but what else do I have to do? *A gal can dream*.

I do a quick check in the mirror by the door. Not bad. At thirty-five, I still look pretty young thanks to staying out of the sun and little to no gray hair. Wearing flattering, dark-wash jeans and a fitted crop top that highlights my figure along with some new eye makeup, I am all about the now. I've even been practicing my flirting skills just in case I meet someone who doesn't seem like a sadist *or* can help me get what I want.

Grabbing my purse, I step out the door and cross the street with a thrill of anticipation for whatever is waiting for me.

Standing in front of the Park MGM, I take a deep breath and soak in the lively scene around me. The energy of the Las Vegas Strip pulses through the air. Across the street, there is a bustling shopping plaza. I can see a Ross Dress for Less, a giant turquoise BrewDog sign, and the Hard Rock Café with its iconic giant electric guitar. Just beside it stands a colossal green Coca-Cola bottle marking the entrance to the Coca-Cola Store, and nearby, the Outback Steakhouse is drawing in hungry tourists. My eyes drift to the New York-New York Hotel and Casino, with its replica of the Empire State Building rising against the backdrop of the desert sky.

But what draws me most is the Dolby Live. The New Soundz will perform there soon, and for the duration of their residency, it will be their home—and, in a way, mine, too. My adrenaline shoots up as I take another moment to inhale the atmosphere. This place will be my future, my present, my everything.

I step inside, and the opulence of the Park MGM's interior takes my breath away. The classy, sophisticated decor envelops me in a sense of indulgence. To my right is Eataly, an Italian marketplace brimming with mouthwatering aromas. Freshly baked pizzas, salty cured hams, and espresso waft from the cafe, which is adorned with glass cases full of pastries so decadent that I make a mental note to try one, maybe even one a day until I've tried them all.

I meander through Eataly, marveling at the array of Italian sweets—crisp biscotti, delicate almond and pistachio cookies, and silky Panna cotta. My mouth waters at the thought of indulging in chocolate truffles from the extravagant chocolate bar, where guests can fill up bags with caramelized, pistachio-dusted, or gold-flecked chocolates. The temptation is almost too much. I'll gain ten pounds here, I think, smiling to myself.

To my left, there is a counter showcasing fresh mozzarella being made right in front of customers, a pizza parlor with wood-fired ovens, a cafe serving Italian street food, and a bar bustling with energy. I can imagine getting lost here, trying everything Eataly offers. What is supposed to be a temporary stay is feeling more like a forever kind of place.

But I have to stay focused. For now, there is only one reason I have come here, but if I am being totally honest, there are two reasons. Ignoring the call of all the food options—I'll have plenty of time for that later—I turn and continue on, passing a vibrant room of slot machines and a noodle restaurant that promises late-night bites. The signs ahead tell me I am close to the Dolby Live.

My heart pounds as I walk up to the theater doors, only to find them locked. Pressing my ear against the solid door, I strain to hear any noise. There is no music, no hint of a soundcheck—just a faint rustling echoing through the space. It's a few weeks before the first show, so maybe they've already finished rehearsing for today, or since it's two in the afternoon, maybe they are at lunch.

Suddenly, the door jiggles, and I jump back in surprise. A man with a tour badge opens the door, looking as startled to see me as I am to see him. He wears thick, nerdy glasses, and his frame is pudgy. His hair is a tousled mess, and I can't help but notice the absence of a wedding ring on his finger.

"Can I help you?"

I try to play it cool. "Oh, I am just seeing if the auditorium is open."

"It's not."

"Oh, okay." I hesitate, then say, "You're working on the residency, right?"

He gives me a curious look, but there is a hint of a smile there. "I am."

I glance at his badge and read the name "Drake." His features soften as he adjusts his glasses. "Are you a fan?" he asks, raising an eyebrow.

"I am but—" I say, trying to sound casual. "I just moved here and am looking for a place to eat. Do you have any recommendations for lunch around here? I'm starving." *Better to downplay my true intentions, right, Rochelle?*

He relaxes a little. "Plenty of great spots, especially right here. They have some killer Italian food."

"You're making my mouth water already," I tease, glancing

down at his badge again. "So, Drake, right? I'm Jess." I hold out my hand, and he takes it, his grip firm but warm.

"Nice to meet you, Jess."

He looks to be around fifty, and as I study his friendly face, a thought sparks in my mind. Maybe, just maybe, Drake can be more than a chance encounter. Maybe he is my ticket into the world I have always dreamed of—the inner circle of the New Soundz. I fantasized for years about being part of that exclusive community, an insider. And now, it seems, I might finally have a chance. *I need that chance.* How hard can it be to win Drake over with my womanly charms? I hope it won't be difficult at all.

I give him my best flirty smile. "Care to join me for lunch? I hate to eat alone."

His cheeks flush. "Sure."

A wave of excitement shoots through me. "Great. Lead the way," I say to him and then think, *Drake, I have a feeling you're going to change my life.*

CHAPTER SIXTEEN

As we walk toward a restaurant with a variety of pasta options, Drake glances at me with a sparkle in his light brown eyes. "The pasta here is my favorite. I'm guessing you like pasta?"

"Love it."

"You're in for a treat." He leads the way, and as we join the queue at the counter, he steps aside to grab a menu for me and hands it over. He is a gentleman, which makes a good impression but a quick flashback to Sam sitting at the bar *and* the next morning reminds me to be cautious.

I study the menu, deliberating over my options. The mushroom fettuccine sounds delicious, but I worry about making a mess while eating it—sauce all over my face or noodles slipping from my fork. Carefully cutting it seems like a lot of work. Maybe the ravioli would be a safer choice—I love ravioli. Decision made, I look up at him. "So, what's good?"

"I'm ordering the fettuccine. It's my favorite."

"I was looking at that, but then I thought maybe the ravioli."

"Trust me, the fettuccine is great."

"All right, I'll get that too," I say, convinced that cutting the noodles isn't actually the end of the world.

After ordering, Drake guides me to a table near the steps, where we can watch the bustling food court scene.

"So, Drake," I begin as we sit down, "you work on the New Soundz residency?"

"I do," he says, while settling into his seat.

"How long have you been in the industry?"

"Thirty years," he says. "I've been a roadie, setting up sound stages, handling logistics, making sure everyone is where they need to be for most of my adult life."

"What are you working on now? Do you do the sound checks and that sort of thing?" I ask, hoping it's a yes and that he can get me into one. More importantly, maybe he can get me backstage. There is *someone* I need to find.

"Not anymore, unless we're short on staff. Now, I pretty much just organize the crew that handles the logistics for the sound checks and rehearsals."

"Wow, it seems like such an exciting job."

"It's all right," he replies with a casual shrug. "I mean, I've gotten to meet a lot of bands."

"What are the New Soundz like?"

"They're good guys."

"I figured." And I did. I don't think any of them have any significant flaws. There was never any bad press or "Me Too" allegations. Not for *them*.

"You're a pretty big fan, aren't you?" he asks, giving me a knowing look.

My heart skips a beat, and I hope he can't see right through me or sense my ulterior motive for striking up a conversation with him. "I was back when I was a teen," I admit. "Actually, I just moved here and saw they're in town. I figure I'll get some tickets."

"I'm sure you can get some," he says with a wink. "I might be able to help you out."

Even though I already have tickets for half the shows, I play along. "That would be amazing!" I gaze into his eyes. "Are you from around here?"

"Oh no. I'm not from here or anywhere, really. It's mostly been a life on the road, and I moved around a lot when I was a kid."

"I understand that." And I do. It's the pits. "Recently, I decided I need a fresh start, somewhere new and exciting. So, I moved here."

He grins. "Well, you'll definitely find plenty of excitement around here. What do you do for work?"

"I was a computer programmer, but I'm taking a break until I figure out what's next. Why—do you need some help on the crew?" I silently plead, *Please, please, please, please, please, please, please.*

He tilts his head, considering. "I mean, we can always use an extra set of hands, but it might not be something you're into. It's a lot of manual labor."

I lift my arm and flex my biceps. "I've got a few muscles here and there. Plus, it could be fun—a part of my new adventure. I'm willing to do *almost* anything."

He chuckles. "I'll look and see what's available, and I'll get back to you. I think we might have a spot for you."

Just then, the waiter sets down heaping plates of fettuccine with creamy sauce and porcini mushrooms. The aroma is heavenly. Without waiting, I dig right in. When I glance up, I notice Drake doing the same, and I feel a little less embarrassed about my eagerness.

"You're right," I say after a few bites, dabbing the corner of my mouth with a napkin. "It's incredible."

"I thought you might like it."

"So, are you off for the rest of the day?"

"There are just a few more things I need to check on to make sure everything's set for tonight's rehearsal."

Between the idea of getting a job with the crew and the possibility of an invitation to the rehearsal, I can barely contain myself. "Do you need my help for that?" I pause, realizing how eager I sound, and try to dial it back. "I mean, if it's not too fast. There's probably paperwork and such. Forget I said anything. I can be patient."

He raises an eyebrow. "Let me check and see what I can do. If I can't get approval for a new position, I might be able to let you listen in on the set. I'm guessing you're hoping to see the New Soundz?"

I grin sheepishly. "Soundling for life." Hopefully, he finds me adorable and not creepy.

He leans forward, his eyes sparkling. "How about this? Let me see if I can get you something part-time. I'll check with the crew, and if it works out, you can come in, meet some folks, and see if it's something you really want to do. And if that coincides with the rehearsal, well... you'll be free to stay for a bit."

My heart nearly jumps out of my chest. I can't believe my luck. "Seriously? Oh my gosh, you're incredible! Thank you so much. This is amazing. I knew coming here was the right decision—and now I've met the nicest person. That's honestly one of the kindest things anyone's ever done for me."

"I'm sorry to hear that, but I'm glad you're excited." He takes another bite of his pasta.

I realize I need to tone down my enthusiasm, so I compose myself and continue eating. After a moment, I say, "What do you do for fun? I mean, I'm guessing it's not all strip clubs and gambling here in Vegas." It's important to learn what he's into if I'm going to get close to him.

"It's not," he says. "There's a lot of great things to do. I love the outdoors, and there's plenty of hiking just outside the city—maybe twenty to thirty minutes away. Plus, we've got the Colorado River, Lake Mead, and recreation areas. And some exhibits at the casinos are really cool."

"Really? I can't wait to see it all."

We continue to chitchat, and I struggle to contain my excitement. Inside, I feel like bouncing off the walls or screaming from the rooftops. I am actually going to see the New Soundz in person! Would it be too much if I wear my old tour jacket? Maybe I should try to play it cool. Just a little.

At the end of our lunch, he says, "I should probably head back. Let me get your number, and I'll let you know if we have anything we need help with."

"Absolutely!" I grab my purse and pull out my phone. He smiles as I hand it to him. "You can add your number, and I'll text you back, if you don't mind, so I'll have your number. I don't know anyone in town, and it sounds like you may have recommendations for places to eat or go out."

"Sure, of course."

I can't help but think, *We're really doing it, Rochelle.* Drake hands my phone back, and I text him.

> Hi! This is Jess. Thank you! 😊

Drake and I finish up lunch, and he says, "What are you up to now?"

"I was just going to wander around the hotel, maybe check out the casino."

"I'll walk with you. I need to head back toward the auditorium."

"Perfect."

We chat about another restaurant in the hotel Drake likes until we reach the auditorium, right outside a bank of slot machines. "All right, this is me. It was great meeting you, Jess. I'll be in touch."

"Thank you so much."

And I watch as Drake pulls out a key to enter. I drag myself away so it doesn't look like I'm staring. I turn toward the slot machines and walk deeper into the casino.

As I walk, I think about waiting around until I hear from him, but I don't want to look like a stalker or like I'm scoping out the place, especially with casino security watching from just about everywhere.

After a loop around the glittering machines and card tables, I make my way back to the slots right outside the auditorium.

An hour later, and a hundred bucks lost to the slot machine gods, the auditorium door creaks open. Drake steps out, accompanied by another man. The newcomer is smaller, with a scruffy five o'clock shadow—probably another crew member. Drake's eyes meet mine, and I freeze. *Busted.*

CHAPTER SEVENTEEN

My heart pounds, but I force a smile and wave. Drake and his friend walk over, their expressions serious. A bead of sweat prickles at the back of my neck.

Over the pings and rings of the slots, Drake says, "You're still here?"

"Oh, yeah," I say, doing my best to sound casual. "These machines are just so... addicting. But I was *just* about to leave."

Drake studies me, his eyes narrowing ever so slightly. "Well, be careful," he says. "They're designed to keep your money."

"I think I've learned that lesson. I'm down quite a bit," I say, forcing a laugh. Hopefully, it doesn't sound psychotic. "That's why I was just about to call it quits."

Drake nods, then gestures to his friend. "This is Gianni. He's part of the crew. Gianni, this is Jess, the one I was telling you about."

He was telling him about me?

Gianni says, "Nice to meet you, Jess."

"Nice to meet you too," I say, extending my clammy hand.

"It's actually a good thing we ran into you," Drake continues. "Gianni's looking for some help in hospitality. It's not exactly high-skilled work. It's mostly setting up tables, organizing the dressing rooms, that kind of thing. It isn't glamorous, but if you're interested, we could use the help."

Gianni says, "I can show you the ropes. We'll be back around six to get everything ready for the rehearsal. Think you can make it?"

I clutch onto the slot machine for balance, my pulse thundering in my ears. "Yes, yes, absolutely! Thank you so much!" My words tumbled out too quickly, but I couldn't help it. "Should I meet you right here?"

Gianni gives me a once over. "Yeah, right by these doors. Six PM. Just wait for me, and I'll come get you."

"Thank you," I say again. "Thank you, Drake. Thank you, Gianni. This is so exciting, and it'll be nice to have a bit of income while I'm here. Especially after my time with these slots."

Drake gives me a long, appraising look. "We can go over logistics when you're in the office later."

"Sure," I say, trying my best to sound composed. "Great! I'm so excited! It's like a dream come true. You two are the best!"

Both men exchange a look, one that makes my stomach twist. I'm coming on too strong, too eager. I have to be more careful. If they get even a whiff of suspicion, I lose everything. I need to blend in, not stand out. *Don't worry, Rochelle, I've got this.*

"Now, I'd better get out of here before this place takes any more of my money." I wave and hurry out of the casino, my shoes pounding loudly against the polished floor. I feel their eyes on my back, a prickle of unease running down my spine. Pushing away the nerves, I focus on the fact that I have gained something great today—a way in. I have a phone number, a name, and a job that will put me close to the New Soundz and their *team*.

Still, I can't shake the way Drake hesitated when he mentioned the job details. Does he suspect something? *I have to play it cool.* No mistakes. I take a deep breath and push through the heavy casino doors, slipping back onto the crowded street, hoping that no one has noticed just how desperately I want this. *Don't worry, Rochelle, soon, I'll get exactly what I came for.*

CHAPTER EIGHTEEN

Inside my suite at the hotel, my nerves are on overdrive. I can't believe I'm going to see them. The New Soundz: Alex, Ethan, Noah, Davey, and Mario.

Rochelle and I were once given the chance to get close to them. We thought we were going to explode with excitement when we got the invitation. It was back when we were kids, and so *very* trusting. The memory takes me back to how that night started.

Rochelle turned to me. "Are you super psyched?"

"So psyched!"

We turned, hand-in-hand, toward the stage, wearing our well-worn matching tour jackets. It was our fourth concert together, but each one felt more exciting than the last. Suddenly the lights went out, and we screamed our hearts out.

When the stage lit up with overhead lighting and pyrotechnics, there they were. I thought I'd faint. The music sounded, and the boys sang my favorite song, *You're My Whole World*.

Rochelle and I jumped up and down before singing along with the band as loud as we could.

Thanks to an epic two-night camp out for tickets with Tina

and Rochelle, we scored floor seats—seventh row. We were so close it was nearly overwhelming. The excitement and utter bliss was something I had never experienced before. The rest of the world fully disappeared in those hours.

During that show, I thought it was the greatest day of my life. I was only fifteen, and there was no way for me to know that. Sadly, it would have been if what happened after the show didn't, in a flash, turn it into the worst.

Pulling myself from the darkness, I jerk out of the memory and back to the present.

In a few hours, I will see them again and even more crazy, I'll be joining their crew, getting in on the inside. *Rochelle, I wish you were here with me.*

Truth be told, I wish she'd been with me all these years. Maybe my life would have turned out differently. Maybe she would have talked me out of marrying Joe. She would have seen him for what he is. She was always a better judge of character than I was. Why couldn't some of her personality have rubbed off on me?

I guess it wasn't meant to be. But that doesn't stop me from wishing she were still right here beside me, about to work backstage.

She should be here for the sound checks and rehearsals, for getting to know the roadies, the stage crew, the lighting guys, and feeling the nervous energy before the show is about to start. But she won't be.

After a deep breath, I think, *Until then, I need to know everything I can about Drake.*

He hasn't given me his last name—just the phone number. But really, that's all I need. A phone number can help find out a lot about a person, assuming the phone is registered to him. It is likely unless he lives at home with his mother and is still on the family plan. That seems unlikely. Then again, you never know anybody, not really.

To keep my mood upbeat, I turn up the sound on my phone, letting the New Soundz music fill the air. I dance and dance as if they're here with me, as if Rochelle is here with me, as if the last twenty years haven't happened and life is full of bliss.

When I am singing their songs and dancing along, I feel transported back to the happy times. Until the dread returns. *No. No. No. Stay away!*

My body heat rises and I feel the sweat prickle. Scolding myself, I think, *You're a grown adult and have more to do than just sing and dance along to the band.*

Ending my impromptu dance session, I sit down on the sofa with my laptop—it is time to get serious.

Back in college, it was a hobby of my fellow programmers to break into different systems and sometimes over the weekends, late at night, we had tournaments to see who could get into secure systems the quickest. I wasn't the best, but I usually placed in the top three. Those late-night parties are about to come in quite handy.

Dusting off my old skills, I search records for Drake's phone number and quickly find the one he put in my phone is registered to a Drake Monaghan. From there, I do a simple search for property records and find his home address and his vehicle information. None of the searches are what one would call legal. Public records show a divorce six years earlier. We have something in common. *Perfect.* I can use that.

I know he will be my ticket to where I need to get to. *Don't you think so, Rochelle?*

With his personal details in mind, I turn my attention to Facebook. He is about the right age to still be active on the platform.

A simple search for Drake Monaghan and a few profiles pop

up. It is the sixth one down when I recognize his face. I click on it. His profile picture shows him with a goldendoodle, and my heart softens. He looks like a nice man—so much nicer than most of the men I've met.

I scroll through his pictures. One is a selfie with a stage in the background. Scrolling through the comments, I learn he worked on a show for a major star who had a Las Vegas residency. Pretty impressive. I click through more pictures, scanning the comments and clicking on his friends' names, peering into their profiles. They all seem to be part of the same world he is in, with multiple photos of concerts, backstage selfies, and events. Drake is deeply entrenched in the music world. *Luck was certainly on my side when I bumped into him.*

He will be tied to the New Soundz for the next two months, and I need to tie myself to him. Not fully healed yet, I'll have to wait a bit to lay on the charm and get closer to Drake—to get closer to my target. But I will. *Eventually.*

Returning to his profile page, I scroll further back. There it is: an announcement that he will be working on the New Soundz' residency in Las Vegas. Standing next to him in the picture is a man with an unsettling smirk that makes my skin prickle.

My body goes hot with rage. My hands ball into fists, and I pound them on the sofa, trying to release the anger that is consuming me.

Deep breaths.

I only have an hour before I will see them again, and I need to be level-headed. Calm. They can't suspect *anything*.

A rattle sounds near the door, and I nearly jump off the sofa. Frozen in place, I strain my ears to catch any sound. Is someone here? Has Drake followed me? Does he know my true intentions? Is he suspicious?

Silence.

I cautiously get off the couch and creep to the door, looking through the peephole. No one is there. Probably just the wind or the air conditioning. Or is paranoia making me edgy?

Returning my focus to Facebook, I try to distract myself by learning more about Drake. A notification pops up: "You're now friends with Drake Monaghan."

My stomach drops. *Oh no*. I accidentally friended him. He's going to think I'm a stalker. Frantically, I unfriend him. But will he get a notification? Will he know? Does it matter that I friended and unfriended him so quickly? Hopefully, he isn't online. I can't friend him—at least, not yet. Panic takes over and I think, *Have I just ruined everything?*

CHAPTER NINETEEN

Pushing down my worries about the Facebook snafu, I walk toward the doors of Dolby Live, and my heart flutters. I am going to be near the same stage where the New Soundz will perform. I will work in the areas where they walk and have conversations. The idea of possibly getting a glimpse of them up close and personal makes my chest tighten with anticipation. Maybe I can even speak to them. I'm sure they're friendly with the crew. *Don't you think so, Rochelle?*

Gianni is there, waiting. He says, "Hello," breaking me from my thoughts.

"Hi."

"Welcome to the team."

"Thank you so much!"

He says, "Come on in," and pushes open the door.

I step inside, my body practically vibrating with anticipation.

"Drake will be out in a few minutes. He's got some paperwork he needs you to fill out, but while we wait, I figured I'd give you a tour."

"Sounds great!" I can't believe this is happening. *I am actually here, working on the New Soundz Las Vegas residency.*

After a rough year—and a lifetime of disappointments, if I'm being honest—I finally feel like things are turning around. This is going to be my happy ending. I have no clue what I will be paid for this job. It probably isn't much, but it doesn't matter. I am here to be close to the New Soundz and their team—even the rotten ones.

Gianni points out the entrances to the backstage area, the stage itself, and the various places where the lighting crew works. My mind can't help but drift back to Rochelle and our brief time backstage. It's what fuels me *and* my rage.

Shoving those thoughts down, I ignore the awful end and pretend it never happened. If it never happened and if we were still best friends, she would be standing beside me, soaking in every moment of this experience. My heart grows heavy. We can't change the past, but I can create a happy ending *with a side order of justice.*

I think Drake will be my way into this world, a means to an end. Is it possible he could be more? He is a little on the older side, like *Joe*. Maybe that is a red flag. Or maybe I can't write off all men of a certain age because of Joe. Or maybe I am thinking too small. Maybe one of the New Soundz members will fall in love with me. I love them all equally, but surely they'll see how much I belong here. I need to do everything I can to impress them, to make them notice me, to make them love me as much as I love them. And more importantly, I need them to trust me.

Gianni finally leads me to a room with a black-painted door. A brass plaque neatly displays Drake's name. *Drake Monaghan.* "That's the end of the tour for now," he says, knocking on the door.

The door swings open, and Drake stands there awkwardly. I spent extra time getting ready. My hair was styled perfectly with a round brush, my makeup meticulously applied to hide any imperfections and remnants of bruising, and I wear a pair of Spanx to look slimmer—assuming that's what he finds attractive.

"You're looking well," I say with a smile.

He blushes. "Thanks. You too. Take a seat."

I pull out a chair across from him, scooting a little closer until my chair is nearly touching his. Drake glances at me with a shy smile and says, "So, we need to add you to the crew officially and make sure you're insured. The crew is covered against any kind of liability or injury. It's standard." He hands me a thick stack of forms. "This isn't your first job, so I'll just let you look through these."

"Thank you so, so much. I really appreciate it." I can't keep the enthusiasm from my voice. Being part of this world is surreal.

"Like I told you, the pay isn't great. You mentioned that wasn't a big deal, so I hope it's still okay."

He shows me the rate, and I try to hide my reaction. It is a tiny fraction of what I used to make as a computer programmer. I make a mental note that I should email my old boss to let her know I quit. That is, if I haven't already been fired for not replying to any of her messages in the past week. "It's fine. At least I'll be making some pocket money. I'm in Vegas, after all, and everything here is so expensive."

"Yes, especially since you're staying on the Strip, right?"

"For now. But I might look for a house or an apartment nearby. I don't have a car, so I figure staying on the Strip will work for now. As long as I'm helping with the tour, I can just walk over." My car is currently parked at the airport in long-term parking. If my stay is for more than a few months, I'll have to go back for it. *No biggie.*

"We have a pretty decent bus system if you ever decide to look for more affordable accommodations."

"I'll think about that. Thank you," I say cheerfully. I feel truly alive, buzzing with energy and hope. It's all because of him—Drake. Being here brought me to him, and it feels like everything is aligning perfectly. *It's all working out, Rochelle.*

We sit together, going over the paperwork. I fill out the forms, signing my name where needed without really reading them. It doesn't matter; what matters is that I am officially becoming part of the New Soundz crew.

Once everything is complete, Drake stands up. "Well, I believe Gianni already gave you the tour, but I'll lead you back. Do you have any questions for me?"

I hesitate, then say, "It sounds like I'll be helping with the catering for the rehearsal tonight. Will they be here? Will I get to see them? Maybe even meet them? Are they... friendly?"

"They'll be here, but we rarely introduce the crew to the band during a rehearsal. But you'll definitely see them."

His smile fades, so I quickly backtrack. "Oh, no big deal. I am just curious, that's all. It's really exciting, but meeting them isn't *everything*." I pause, then add, "I mean, I did get to meet you and that's pretty great."

His cheeks turn rosy. He likes me. This could be something much bigger than I ever imagined. Drake is the kind of man I should be with: caring, generous, and sweet. But didn't I think that of Joe in the beginning too?

Could Drake be different? Would I have to watch my weight and always do my hair and makeup to look my best or he'd not be interested? Well, that test can come later. But considering I am having fun dressing up, especially now that I have a reason, it's not a big deal yet.

Drake says, "Okay, let me show you back."

I follow him, wondering if there is some unspoken rule about dating the crew. Probably not. This isn't corporate America, after all. I resolve to try not to come on too strong. I've never been the aggressive type, but that is all changing. Jessica—the meek, quiet version of me who tries to please everyone—is gone. I am Jess, and when I want something, I go for it.

Gianni stands nearby, clipboard in hand, looking ready to assign me my first tasks. I wave to him and turn back to Drake. I lightly touch his arm and say, "Thanks again. *Really*." Then I force myself to focus on the job, reminding myself that I need to prove my worth here. I can't afford to lose this opportunity—or my chance to be close to the New Soundz and the main reason I came to Vegas. *I can't lose sight of my plan.*

CHAPTER TWENTY

My new job is surprisingly fun, like setting up for a party, a wedding, or some other big event. The air buzzes with excitement as people bustle around, each with a task to do. Although the catering hasn't arrived, the tables are set up and decorated. Elegant vases hold perfectly arranged flowers, adding a touch of beauty to the scene.

Gianni hands me another vase of flowers. "These go into Mario's dressing room, right over there."

Shock nearly takes over. *Mario's dressing room.* With my heart pounding, I enter the dressing room and set the flowers on the coffee table in front of a sleek leather sofa. Mirrors line one wall of the tastefully decorated room, which also contains a chair and a desk, probably used for hair and makeup. Does Mario wear makeup? I'm not sure. Probably. As I stand there, taking it all in, it feels unreal. I want to stay forever, just soaking up the atmosphere.

Unable to help myself, I lift one of the couch pillows and sniff it. It smells of clean fabric, no trace of Mario. Maybe he hasn't been in yet. A sudden noise makes me jump.

Footsteps echo down the hallway, and I quickly put the

pillow back, smoothing it over as I step out of the room. I pause on the threshold, glancing back for one last look. I am so close, so close to a member of the band. *Can you believe it, Rochelle?*

Drake is only a few feet away, so I scramble out and shut the door behind me.

"How's your first day going?" he asks.

"Pretty good! Gianni's a great teacher," I say with a huge smile. "We've got the tables set up, and we're just waiting on catering. Everything's coming together."

Drake's eyes twinkle. "You're not too bored, are you?"

"Not at all."

"Great. Let me know if you need anything."

"Well, I don't really need anything, but... I'm just so grateful for this opportunity." I pause, then say, "Can I thank you by taking you to dinner this week?"

A blush creeps up Drake's neck. "I'd like that."

"Great!"

"All right then," he says with a slight grin.

My face hurts from smiling so much, but I can't help it. This is an incredible turn of events. Drake tells me he has to get back to his office, and I wink at him as he walks past. That's right. I'm Jess now, and I go after what I want. And there are definitely things I want.

As Drake disappears, I can't resist the urge to explore a bit. I want to know where all the secret entrances and exits are or at least get a sense of the best places to stay unseen. Knowing where the cameras are located could come in handy, too. I wander down the hallway—one of the few places Gianni hasn't shown me. The hall isn't well lit. There are a few unmarked doors and some with official nameplates.

My body tenses as I read one name, and a rush of anger floods through me. I clench my hands into fists, my cheeks burning and my body breaking out in a light sweat. Memories and emotions I tried hard to suppress threaten to burst free. Memories that nearly *destroyed* me.

"Jess!" Gianni's voice snaps me back to reality.

I spin around, forcing my expression back to neutral.

"What are you doing down there?" he asks, eyeing me with a hint of suspicion.

"I think I got turned around."

He seems unfazed. "No need to be down here. These are the executive offices for the bigwigs who run the residency. You don't need to worry about them."

"Right, of course. Thank you," I say, my cheerful demeanor snapping back into place. "Has catering gotten here yet?"

"They just texted. They'll be here in five minutes. Time to roll up our sleeves."

"Consider them rolled up!"

I follow him back to the main area, determined to push away the dark thoughts and focus on the present—*on the mission*.

The band will arrive soon for the rehearsal, and I need to stay focused and under the radar. Drake, or any of the others, can't know my true intentions. If they find out, it could ruin everything, and I can't handle another defeat of that magnitude. It would surely break me into a thousand pieces—too many pieces to be put back together again.

CHAPTER TWENTY-ONE

Everything is ready for the New Soundz to arrive for the rehearsal. I've learned they've been rehearsing for the past few weeks and only have a few left before the soundcheck and the first show.

As instructed, I stand by the catering table, ready to assist anyone needing a napkin, fork, or anything else. In a few moments, the New Soundz will arrive, and I am practically bursting with excitement. It feels as though all the pain and heartbreak I endured have led me to this moment, one filled with joy and hope and purpose.

I am part of their world now. Not just a fan, but a member of the New Soundz community. If you told me just a few weeks ago that I'd end up here, I would have laughed. I was trapped in a life full of dreariness, rejection, and lingering hurt from Joe's betrayal. But now here I am, free and brand-new. I finally belong, and happiness is once again within my reach. Not just happiness, but I also have a purpose. I can have both. I've never had both.

Gianni rushes over, his face alight with urgency. "They're here."

Stunned, I feel my heart race, pounding so hard that I wonder if it might leap right out of my chest. *They're here.*

"What should I do?" I ask, trying to contain the tremor in my voice.

Gianni says, "Well, they may go into their dressing rooms first. Just make sure that if they come out and want any snacks, you're here to help them."

"So... I might meet them?"

"Most likely," Gianni says with a knowing smile. "But don't be pushy. Don't act like too much of a fan—you know what I mean. Be low key. Just offer any service they might need and just be yourself. You'll be fine."

"Will do," I say, although I am trembling with nerves and excitement. I want to shout out loud that I am finally here, that this dream is real. I wish Rochelle was with me, like she was at those concerts all those years ago when we held hands, screaming and jumping up and down when the band took the stage. That isn't possible, so I promised her that I would do this for the both of us.

The memories flood back, and I silently blame my mother for Rochelle leaving my life. When my mother moved me away, Rochelle and I lost the closeness of seeing each other at school every day. We lived too far apart to visit often. If I'd stayed, if I was there for her, maybe things would have turned out differently. Maybe she'd be standing here with me, about to meet the band. It *should* be both of us.

Voices and laughter pull me from my thoughts, and I turn to see them. My jaw drops. Alex, Ethan, Noah, Davey, and Mario are walking toward the catering area, laughing and joking, nudging one another playfully. They are right here, real and vibrant, just a few feet away from me.

Noah calls out, "I'm going to head to my dressing room, but then I might grab a bite before we hit the stage. Cool?"

I can't believe it. My idols, the people I admired for so long, are right in front of me. I force myself to breathe and stay calm, ready to make a good impression. This is my moment—my chance to be close to them.

The other guys give Noah a nod before retreating to their dressing rooms, leaving just one member lingering by the catering table. Davey, the band's resident "bad boy," is right in front of me. Back in the day, he wore ripped jeans and several layered necklaces, oozing charisma with every casual movement. I know his persona is just that—a persona. He's never really been a bad boy. According to the internet, he is happily married to an actress and has a few kids. He looks incredible in dark wash denim and a black T-shirt. They all do. In their mid-forties, the band members have somehow maintained their youthful magnetic energy.

Davey looks right at me, and my heart nearly stops. "Hi," he says, flashing that famous smile.

I swallow hard, willing myself to act normal. "Hi. I'm Jess. I'm with hospitality. Is there anything I can get you?" My voice shakes with excitement. The moment is almost too much to handle. I never imagined I'd be speaking to *Davey*.

"Nice to meet you, Jess. What've you got today? I'm starved."

Rochelle, he said my name! Mustering every ounce of composure in me, I launch into a description of the different food options, my words tumbling out quickly. "If there's anything you want but we don't have, I can run and get it for you right away. Anything at all." I mean it—anything for him. He smiles and lets out a small chuckle that makes my knees feel weak.

"I don't think I've seen you before. How long have you been with the crew?" he asks. "Are you from Las Vegas?"

He is asking about me—*me*. I almost can't contain my giddiness. Are we having an actual conversation? Will we become friends? The thought makes me explode with joy. "I just started today," I say, trying to keep my voice steady. "And I just moved to Las Vegas. I'm from California. I used to be a computer programmer, but you know, life has lots of twists and turns, and I ended up here. When I was a kid, I went to four of your concerts with my best friend. I even still have my old tour jacket." I silence myself. Was that too much?

"That's incredible," Davey says, his eyes lighting up. "Well, welcome aboard. And thank you. This looks great."

Floating, I say, "And if you need any beverages we don't have here, just let me know. We've tried to stock all the band's favorites, but in Vegas, you can get anything you want in a heartbeat."

"I appreciate it, but this all looks pretty good. Oh, and my wife might stop by later. If she comes in, could you let her know where my dressing room is?"

"Absolutely."

"Thanks, Jess."

As he fills his plate, I swear a feather could knock me over. *He remembered my name.*

If this happened twenty years ago, I would have turned to Rochelle, and we would have screamed and jumped up and down, marveling that Davey knew my name. But now, I stand alone, smiling like an idiot, barely able to contain the energy that threatens to burst out of me.

Davey finishes filling his plate of food, grabs a bottle of water, and heads to his dressing room. I watch him go, still in disbelief. I helped Davey from the New Soundz. It's a dream come true.

Gianni walks over, a knowing grin on his face. "So, how'd it go?"

I can barely contain myself. "I helped Davey get some food. He said he was starving."

"Great. That must've been pretty cool for you."

"It really was," I say, my voice soft with awe. "You know, sometimes life kicks you down to the curb, but then you make a change, climb back up, and suddenly the sun shines even brighter than before."

He eyes me. "True."

Just as I am catching my breath from meeting Davey, Mario approaches the table. My pulse quickens, but I take a deep breath and remind myself to stay composed. This is Mario—the oldest member of the New Soundz, the studious one who wore glasses in the early days, though he isn't wearing them now. Like the others, he is in great shape, tall with striking salt-and-pepper hair. He is everything I imagined and more.

"Hi," I say, not waiting for him to greet me first, like Davey did.

"Hi there," he says, with a friendly smile. "This all looks pretty good. Any recommendations? Nothing too heavy."

My heart does a little flip. Mario is standing right in front of me, asking for food recommendations. "The enchiladas look amazing. Chicken, not too much cheese," I say, gesturing to the steaming trays. "I haven't had them myself yet, but I've heard they're great."

"Well, maybe I'll give those a try," he says with a thoughtful nod. "I love enchiladas."

Of course he does. Everything on the table is meticulously selected to match the band members' tastes.

As Mario fixes his plate, I ask, "Is there anything else I can get for you?"

"I'm good, thanks." He isn't quite as chatty as Davey was, but I tell myself he is just more reserved. It doesn't mean he is dismissive or unkind. He is Mario, after all—a good guy, just like the rest of them. I believe that with all my heart.

But something is different about him—not jovial like the others. It's as if he is haunted. Maybe despite his fame, he is going through some personal things. You never really know what someone's going through. I'll be sure to be extra helpful to him, if I can.

Next, I meet Noah. The soulful, quiet one. He is also married and in his forties, but that doesn't make him any less breathtaking. He is charming, with a theater-honed smile that can light up the room. Noah even asks my name and where I am from, listening attentively as I tell him a little about myself. These men really are the best. *We were right about them, Rochelle.*

While I am chatting with Noah, Alex approaches, and Noah introduces us. My heart swells as Noah says my name. He even explains to Alex that I've been living in California. Alex is one of the most popular too—with his high-pitched ballads and sexy persona. Even now he wears black skinny jeans and a button-down white shirt with a few extra unbuttoned, showing off his dark chest hair. From what I've read, he's single.

Alex's face lights up. "California? No way. I used to live in Southern California."

"Really? I'm from Northern California. The Bay Area."

"California's great, isn't it? I miss it already."

I can barely believe it. Here I am, talking about California with Alex. These are the greatest guys in the world. I always thought so, but now I truly know it. Standing there having conversations with them proves they are worthy of my decades of admiration.

Then comes Ethan, the youngest of the band members, though he has long since grown into a full-fledged man. His big blue eyes are just as bright as ever. He approaches with an easy smile. "Any chance you've got a Coke or maybe an espresso? I need a jolt of energy."

I step forward eagerly. "We have both! I can make you a fresh espresso. We have a machine."

Ethan grins and gives me a playful wink. "Espresso sounds perfect. Coke too."

"Absolutely," I say, trying not to let my voice shake. "The Coke's on the table, and I'll make the espresso right now."

As I prepare his drink, my hands shake lightly. I am making espresso for Ethan. I wish I had someone to call, someone who understands how monumental this is, but there is no one. Sometimes life works out that way—you achieve dreams you don't even know you have, and then there is no one to share it with. But I tell myself to savor it anyway. And that can change. I could have a best friend or a partner again. *I have to believe that.*

The espresso machine beeps, and I carefully hand the small cup and saucer to Ethan, fighting the urge to scream like a teenage girl.

"I'm Jess. I'm new, but anything you need, I'm here for you."

Ethan takes the cup and smiles. "Thanks, Jess. I'm Ethan."

"I know," I blurt out, my cheeks flushing. "I was your biggest fan back in the day."

He laughs, a warm, genuine sound that makes me think it'll make me burst. "I'm glad you're still with us."

"I even still have my fan club membership card. Soundling for life," I add, feeling a little ridiculous but too excited to care. "I just found it recently. Isn't that funny?"

"That's awesome," he says. "Well, thanks for the espresso. Hope you enjoy the show. You will be listening, right?"

"Definitely."

Ethan smiles one last time before heading off, and I stand there, a grin stretched so wide that my face hurts. I did it. I made an impression, however small, and it is everything I ever dreamed of.

I feel like I could melt right here on the floor. These guys, the New Soundz, actually talked to me, and I am part of their world now. I feel unstoppable, like nothing can go wrong, and I promise myself I will make sure it doesn't.

As the band members make their way to their dressing rooms to prepare for the sound check, I turn around to see Drake standing nearby. He must have been there the whole time, witnessing my interactions with the band.

He approaches.

"You said I probably wouldn't meet them," I say, my voice still filled with awe.

"Sometimes they don't come out before rehearsal, but I'm glad you got to meet them. Looks like they made your day."

"My day? Yeah, they definitely made my day." I look at him, feeling a surge of gratitude. "And it's all because of you!" Before I can think better of it, I step forward and wrap my arms around him, giving him a spontaneous hug.

As soon as I realize what I've done, I pull back, mortified. "Oh my gosh, I'm so sorry. That is so inappropriate. I'm just so overwhelmed. Everything's been a whirlwind today, and I'm just... so grateful."

Drake's eyes soften. "I'm glad you're happy."

Footsteps echo down the hall, and I instinctively glance over, hoping it's one of the New Soundz returning. But it isn't. It is a man of about sixty, with tight jeans and a fitted T-shirt. The sight of him makes my skin crawl. He oozes *ick*.

Drake turns to greet the newcomer. "Hey, Ricky. How's it going?"

The man—Ricky—smiles and gives a casual nod. "It's going well. Everything ready for tonight?"

"Yes, sir," Drake says, then gestures to me. "This is Jess.

She's working in hospitality. Anything you need, she can help you out."

Ricky turns his gaze to me, his smile forced. "Nice to meet you, Jess. Welcome aboard. Hopefully, you'll be with us for the whole residency."

Through gritted teeth, I say, "Thank you. I'm looking forward to it."

"Great. I'm just going to grab a bite and head back to my office." He picks up some chips and guacamole, tips his head in a polite farewell, and walks away.

I watch him go, my smile frozen in place.

On the outside, he's nice, polite. I know his type. What he is capable of. And I know it's all a facade. Inside, he is rotten—filled with maggots and flesh-eating bugs, a core of decay hidden beneath a veneer of normalcy. I clench my fists at my sides, knowing Ricky is a monster. A monster I *will* destroy.

CHAPTER TWENTY-TWO

WHILE THE BAND PLAYS, I stand awestruck by the catering table. They sound incredible, performing their most popular songs. The music transports me to a place of love and happiness —screaming at the top of my lungs, tears streaming down my face, Rochelle and I hugging, dancing, and singing along to every word.

When the band wraps for the night, it feels like a heaviness settles down over the room. The sound fades, leaving behind a stillness—a chaotic energy replaced by a dark, quiet place. My thoughts turn dark as well.

The memory of one of the last letters I ever received from Rochelle.

The paper she wrote on had faint watermarks and smudged ink, and I realized she'd cried while writing it. Her despair ripped through me and all I wanted to do was help her, be there for her, but I couldn't get to her. After a second read-through of the letter, I ran to the phone to call her. As the ring tone sounded over and over, her voicemail clicked on. Three more tries and I knew she wouldn't answer. My body filled with dread and anger. I was trapped, not able to fix it. Helpless. I screamed and screamed until my sister ran in to see what was happening. She placed her small hand on my back, and I crumbled to the floor, embracing the then seven-year-old. She stroked my hair. "It's okay, sissy. It's okay."

Nodding, I quieted, not wanting to scare Lucy any more than I already had.

The sound of the band knocks me out of the memory as they come rushing through, their laughter and chatter filling the backstage hallway. I brush the lone tear from the corner of my eye and then smile while I tell them they sounded great—because they did. They always did. I wait patiently, seeing if anyone needs anything before helping with the cleanup.

When most of the crew has gone home and we've finished tidying up, the venue falls silent. Drake must be in his office, and I know Gianni has taken the trash to the dumpsters outside. I realize it might be my only chance to get inside Ricky's office.

The darkened hallway feels longer than usual as I make my way down it. Ricky's office door is slightly ajar. I slip inside, pulling out my phone flashlight to guide me. The office is surprisingly large, though I suppose it makes sense. Ricky Star isn't just the tour manager for the band's Las Vegas residency. He also managed their tours back in the day. It's strange to me that they kept him around.

I creep around the room. A desk, a sofa, his own private bathroom—complete with a shower, tub, and vanity. It feels more like a tiny apartment. He could live here if he wanted to.

Nothing seems out of the ordinary. It doesn't look like anyone has used the office recently. But I am not looking for ordinary. I am looking for something—anything—that can prove Ricky is the monster I know he is.

I've seen that look in his eyes before, and I know what men like him are capable of. Ricky's dark deeds could tarnish the band's name forever. With all the #MeToo revelations, it surprises me no one has come forward yet.

Creeping over to the desk, I open the drawers. I shuffle through papers, a pair of reading glasses, and a tube of ChapStick—nothing unusual. In the bottom drawer, I am shocked to find a small gun. It's black with a wooden handle. A revolver. I don't know much about guns, but it looks older. Maybe a collector's item. But if it's an antique, why isn't it displayed on a shelf instead of hiding in a drawer?

Why would Ricky keep a gun in his desk? It feels out of place. I've read Vegas can be dangerous, but this doesn't sit right with me. Of all people, I don't want Ricky Star in possession of a deadly weapon. Without thinking another thought about it, I slip the gun into my jeans, covering it with my flowing top.

My pulse races when I hear footsteps approaching—heading toward the office. I hastily close the drawer, glancing around the room for an escape. Where can I go? My eyes dart to the sofa, and I skitter behind it, crouching low. My breath hitches as the door creaks open.

The overhead light flicks on, and I hope whoever has entered can't hear the pounding of my heart. With my hand over my mouth, trying to suppress any sound, I press myself against the back of the sofa and try to make myself as small as possible.

CHAPTER TWENTY-THREE

My heart beats a million times per minute as I crouch behind the sofa, praying they won't see me. If they find me, I can't explain why I'm here, and they'll likely fire me from the crew. My mind races, scrambling for a believable excuse, but nothing convincing comes to mind.

The space behind the sofa is just big enough to conceal me, but I have to be careful. If I make a sound, or even breathe too heavily, I could give myself away. My heart pounds so loudly in my ears I'm sure they'll hear it.

Footsteps approach the desk—two sets. I can't risk peeking to see who it is, so I press myself tighter against the sofa, hoping the shadows and silence will keep me hidden.

One voice breaks the silence. "Nice work out there."

"Thanks, Ricky. Now, what is this about? You're the one who said you wanted to talk."

I recognize the voices. It's Ricky and Mario. Something about their tone sets me on edge.

"I want to make sure you know to keep quiet," Ricky says, his voice low and menacing.

Mario's response is sharp. "I've been quiet this long. What makes you think I'm going to talk now?"

Ricky chuckles darkly. "You were young back then. Now, you seem to be... open about everything—your life, your *lifestyle*. I just want to remind you I have ways of making your life a living hell if you ever decide to grow a conscience."

"You have nothing to worry about," Mario says evenly, though there's tension in his voice.

"Good," Ricky says. "Because I still have a lot of friends in the industry, and I can still destroy you. Don't forget that."

"Are we done here?"

"Don't forget what I said."

Footsteps retreat, the sound growing softer as they leave the office. I stay crouched, still hidden, as my mind struggles to process what I've overheard.

What does Mario know? Why is Ricky threatening him?

Does Mario know about Ricky's crimes? My heart sinks with disappointment at the thought that Mario is complicit. Shaking my head, I can't make sense of it. If Mario knows Ricky is a monster, why hasn't he said anything?

Ricky's threats, Mario's guarded tone, and the unspoken history between them might point to something bigger. I need to find out exactly what Mario is hiding for Ricky and whether Mario is involved in Ricky's crimes—assuming I can get out of the office without being fired. Ricky paces before shutting off the lights and exiting the office, closing the door behind him.

I'm shaken by the implication—could Mario be as rotten as Ricky? *Rochelle, tell me it isn't so!*

CHAPTER TWENTY-FOUR

THE COAST SEEMS CLEAR, but I can't be sure Ricky and Mario have left yet. I step into the hall near the dressing rooms, and Gianni appears. "Where were you?"

Thinking quick, I say, "I was just checking to see if Ricky needed anything else before I left." My stomach clenches, hoping he can't see through my lie—or worse, notice what I have tucked into the front of my jeans under my top.

Gianni raises a brow but doesn't press further. "Okay... usually we don't do that. Is he still here?"

I shake my head quickly. "The lights in his office are off."

"Well, we're just about done here. Nice work today," he says, offering a small nod of approval.

"Thanks, Gianni." I glance around, feigning casualness. "Is anyone else still here?"

"I'm not sure."

I hesitate, then add, "I thought I heard someone earlier. Maybe I should check to see if they need anything?"

"I don't think that's necessary," he says, studying me as though trying to figure out if my demeanor is suspicious.

"It's no problem. I don't mind." Ricky and Mario were there

just five minutes ago. They could easily still be around, and I would love to talk to Mario.

"It's fine. I'll handle it. You go home. Have a good night, Jess."

"Thank you again for the job. It's great. Have a good night," I say with what I hope is a convincing smile.

Gianni watches as I gather my purse. Trying not to seem fazed, I wave as I head toward the outside exit.

Walking toward the door, I feel his eyes on me.

The way Gianni looks at me, I know I need to be more careful. I push through the backstage exit and step outside into the cool night air. The Strip's lights cast everything in a vibrant glow. I linger outside in the alley, unsure of my next move. My hotel is only a short walk across the street, but something makes me hesitate. Is Mario still inside? Will he exit through this door? I have no idea where he's staying or if he's going out for a late night.

Deciding to wait, I pull out my phone, pretending to scroll, trying to appear as though I have a reason to stand around in a dark alley outside the parking garage by myself.

The door opens, and my heart leaps into my throat. Then it sinks just as quickly.

"What are you still doing here?" Gianni asks.

Great, not who I'm hoping to bump into. "I'm just texting a friend," I say, holding up my phone with what I hope is a convincing look.

He eyes me for a moment. "Okay. Good night."

"Good night," I say, trying to sound chipper and not like I've just been caught.

As soon as he turns away, I pretend to type furiously on my phone, maintaining the act in case he looks back at me. I can't let Gianni suspect me any more than he already does.

While I'm there, I decide to check social media and finally

email my workplace and give them my official resignation. *With a few taps, it's done.* It feels great to have that checked off my list of things to do.

A few minutes later, the door creaks open again. My chest tightens, and I brace myself for who might walk out next. My body tenses as one of the lighting technicians walks out casually. They don't seem to recognize me, so I focus on my phone to avoid any unnecessary conversations.

As soon as they disappear toward the garage, I exhale.

I shouldn't be standing so close to the door—it's a little odd. I take a few paces toward the garage to look less like I'm waiting for someone.

As I stare at the tiny screen, thoughts of Rochelle rush in. *That night.* The night that changed everything.

When I pulled the New Soundz tour jacket from that box, I was taken back to a time of friendship, love, and belonging. That's what I associate with the New Soundz. When the nurse mentioned the residency, I thought maybe I could reclaim those old feelings, but I know I can't—because I recall why it all ended. I can't just go back to that... not without making things right. Once things are right, and Ricky is destroyed, I can reclaim the joy that is the New Soundz community. *Soundlings for life, right, Rochelle?*

Lost in my thoughts, I barely notice the other crew members who exit from time to time. Lost in dark thoughts and the late hour approaching, I'm ready to head back to my suite. As I begin my trek back, the door opens, and he steps outside.

Our eyes lock.

Mario.

I want to launch into small talk, but the look in his eyes stops me in my tracks. He looks weary, as if the weight of whatever he's hiding has been crushing him for years. Unlike the other band members—who seem upbeat and friendly—Mario is guarded, distant. I think I understand why. Maybe he just needs someone to talk to. I can be that someone.

"Still here?" he asks.

I step closer to him, trying to keep my voice steady. "I'm waiting for a friend."

He shrugs. "All right. See you later."

This is my moment. I have to take it. "Hey, wait."

Mario stops and looks at me.

"I'm a big fan. I used to go to all your concerts when I was a teen." I pause, searching his face for any sign of approval. "My best friend and I went to four concerts of yours."

He says, "Thanks. I appreciate that. Have a good night," and starts to walk away.

The air feels tense, like he's just being polite but doesn't want to talk. Well, he's not getting off that easy. I raise my voice, "My friend Rochelle and I—we even got backstage once. Ricky approached us after a show. He offered to take us backstage to meet you."

Mario stops.

He knows.

I approach him and our eyes meet. "We didn't meet you though."

His jaw clenches.

"But you probably know that. Was that his MO? How he preyed on young girls?"

Even in the dim light, I see his face blanch.

"You knew. You knew what happened to Rochelle. How many others? Why would you cover for him? He's a monster!"

"I don't know what you're talking about," he says stiffly, his voice barely above a whisper.

"You do," I say, my voice rising as tears begin streaming down my face. "You know what Ricky is. You know what he's done. Why would you hide it? Why would you protect him? Why?"

"I'm sorry," Mario says, his words hollow. "But I don't know what you're talking about."

He turns on his heel and hurries off, leaving me standing there in the cold night, tears blurring the neon lights of the Las Vegas Strip. How can he do that?

He knows what Ricky has done—not just to Rochelle but to others; I'm sure of it. And yet he stays silent, year after year, allowing Ricky to continue.

Why?

I slide down the wall, my legs giving out beneath me as I bury my face in my hands. The weight of it all crashes over me like a tidal wave.

How many have there been after Rochelle—or before? How many more could have been saved if he had spoken up? If *I* had spoken up?

CHAPTER TWENTY-FIVE

INSIDE MY HOTEL SUITE, I dry my eyes as I pace the floor, my mind spinning as I try to process the whirlwind of a day. Meeting my heroes had been incredible—unreal even. The sound of their voices singing on stage during the rehearsal plays in my mind, and for a moment, I allow myself to savor the memory. Work was fun and everyone was nice, but then there was *Ricky*. And Mario. And the *gun*.

Staring at the gun in my hand, I realize I don't know what I should do with it. I took it, but I wasn't even sure why. What am I going to do if housekeeping comes into my suite and sees it?

My eyes dart around the room and stop on the nightstand. I dart into the bedroom and pull open the drawer. Inside sits a Bible, and I think I can hide it here, but is that sacrilegious? I'm not sure, but I don't want to debate ethics so I place the gun next to the book. Staring at it for a moment, I realize it looks too exposed and I need to cover it. But before that, I snap a photo with my phone in case of... *I don't know what*. Maybe I'll do a Google search to learn more about it. Satisfied, I go into the bathroom and grab a hand towel and bring it into the room and place it on top of the gun. *Better,* I think.

With a quick click, the drawer shuts closed, and I walk back into the living room.

That's squared away for the moment. Now there is the matter of Mario. He nearly crushed me with his denial. I know he wasn't telling me the truth. He knows what Ricky has done. He's probably known for years and hasn't told anyone. That is the part I can't understand.

Thinking back to the conversation I overheard in Ricky's office, Ricky had said something to the effect of, "You're very open now, but I could still destroy you." It was clear Ricky had leverage over Mario, but what?

And then it hit me.

Twenty years ago, Mario wasn't out as a gay man. He had a string of high-profile celebrity girlfriends. Times were different then; being gay could have destroyed his career. Was that why he kept Ricky's secrets all these years? Had Ricky been blackmailing him this whole time?

If that was true, why wouldn't Mario come forward now? Why wouldn't he talk to me and explain everything? I feel gutted by his betrayal. Mario let Ricky's crimes remain hidden, let him continue on without consequence. Ricky had destroyed Rochelle's life, and Mario—*Mario had stayed silent.*

I feel sick as memories of that night come flooding back. Once, what we shared—the New Soundz community—had been beautiful, a utopia for people like us. But Ricky poisoned it.

That night, Rochelle and I were just two teenage girls high on seeing their favorite band. The painful memories flash forward.

It was after the concert. Most of the crowd had already left, the lights dimmed, the stage cleared. But we stayed behind, hanging out near the edge of the stage. We weren't ready to leave, not yet. We wanted to be close to the magic, even if the band was gone. Rochelle said, "Can you believe we're touching the stage where Alex, Ethan, Noah, Davey, and Mario stood? Their shoes were right here!" Her eyes were wide and filled with excitement.

That was when an older man came walking toward us. He'd come from backstage, and we were thrilled just to be close to someone—anyone—who went backstage. Rochelle and I held hands, trying to contain our excitement as he approached us and said, "Still here?"

We both nodded quickly, giddy that someone—anyone—associated with the New Soundz was talking to us.

"You must be pretty big fans," he said, his voice sounding kind.

"The biggest fans. Soundlings for life," Rochelle said with a wide grin.

"It's true—we've gone to all their concerts in the Bay Area," I added.

"Well," he said, his tone casual, "I suppose you'd love to meet the guys."

Rochelle said, "For sure!"

He gave a coy smile. "I could get you backstage."

My eyes widened. "Are you serious?"

"But you have to be cool," he added, his gaze shifting between us. "They don't like it when fans are screaming and jumping up and down. You guys are cool, right?"

"Oh, yeah, totally," Rochelle said, radiating confidence. "We're not like some of those screaming kids out here. We're *eighteen*."

I cringed inwardly at the obvious lie, but it didn't seem to faze him. His lips curled into a sly smile.

"Well then," he said, gesturing for us to follow. "Let's see if they're still here. Come on. I'm Ricky. I'm the tour manager."

My heart pounded as he waved us toward the entrance to

backstage. Rochelle and I clutched hands tightly together as we followed behind Ricky.

Backstage was quieter than I'd expected. The buzz of the concert was gone, replaced by a quiet stillness. A few scattered cables and empty soda cans lay on a table and one on the ground.

Ricky stopped and turned toward us. "I don't want to overwhelm them since they aren't expecting any fans right now," he said smoothly. "What are your names?"

"I'm Jessica."

"And I'm Rochelle."

"All right, Rochelle, why don't you come with me? Jessica, you stay here. It'll only be a few minutes. Is that okay? I just want to make sure we don't make them feel like they're being bombarded."

My gut churned, warning me that this wasn't normal. Something about this didn't sit right with me. "Really? Us overwhelm them? We can just go together," I said, trying to change his mind.

Ricky's demeanor shifted. His tone hardened, though he kept his smile. "Just stay here. I promise we won't be long."

Rochelle turned to me, her eyes sparkling with anticipation. "It's okay," she reassured me. "We're going to meet them. It's going to be awesome. Don't worry—you always worry too much!"

I hesitated but eventually nodded. Rochelle was usually a good judge of character and she seemed so sure of herself. How could I say no? Rochelle's life hadn't been without turbulence, but she hadn't encountered the type of men I had. Men who were "friends" of my mother. Men who didn't care if a girl was underage or had begged them to stop.

Ricky said, "Don't worry, Jessica. We'll be right back."

Rochelle waved, and I could tell she was practically bursting with anticipation.

After a quick wave, I sank into a worn leather sofa and watched as they started to walk away.

And then they were gone.

The silence grew heavy. Minutes stretched into what felt like hours. Something was wrong—I could feel it in my bones—but I didn't know what to do. I didn't have a cell phone and couldn't call for help. While I waited, not a single person appeared. Maybe Rochelle's mom would get suspicious and come looking for us. Rochelle had called her earlier asking for a little more time—twenty minutes, she'd pleaded—to hang out in the stadium to soak up the vibe.

As I sat there, my mind raced but my body was paralyzed.

When they finally returned, Rochelle wouldn't meet my eyes. Her hair hung like a curtain around her face, and she stared at the floor, trembling. Ricky's voice broke the silence.

"Well, we looked everywhere, but they're not here. Sorry, maybe next time."

"Where did you go looking? You've been gone a *long* time."

"Don't be ridiculous," Ricky snapped. "It's only been twenty minutes. When you're older, you'll learn patience." He moved to the side door and held it open, ushering us out.

I climbed off the couch and hurried after Rochelle. Something was wrong—I could see it in the way her shoulders slumped, the tears glistening in her eyes. She was pale, her movements unsteady.

I whispered, "What happened?"

"Let's go," she said, her voice tight. "Let's just go, okay? My mom's waiting for us outside."

"What did he do?" I asked, dread curling in my stomach.

She finally looked at me, her eyes hollow, her expression haunted. "Let's just go."

I nodded numbly, swallowing the lump in my throat.

She was silent the rest of the night.

It was weeks before Rochelle would tell me what Ricky had done to her. She cried as she explained how she had begged him to stop and that she didn't want to do *that*. Ricky didn't care. He then smashed his hand over her mouth to muffle her cries until he finished stealing her virginity.

It was the last concert we ever attended together. We never listened to or sang along or danced to their music ever again.

That night marked the end of everything—our childhood, our joy, the bond we had built. Nothing was ever the same.

After that, Rochelle withdrew into herself, and I had spent years replaying that moment over and over, wishing I could change it. I knew something was off about Ricky. Maybe if I'd followed my gut, maybe if I hadn't let fear hold me back, I could have stopped it. But I didn't. That guilt has haunted me ever since. *I'm so sorry, Rochelle. I'm going to make it right, as right as I can.*

How would Rochelle feel if she found out that Mario knew about Ricky? That he stayed silent about what Ricky did—maybe he didn't know what happened to Rochelle, but there had to have been other girls. Of that, I'm sure. Girls as gullible as we were, suckered in by the promise of meeting the New Soundz. Those girls' voices need to be heard. All of them, not just Rochelle's. And I am going to make that happen, *one way or another*.

CHAPTER TWENTY-SIX

IT IS ALMOST midnight and I'm exhausted. In less than twenty-four hours, I've moved to Las Vegas, landed a job, met the New Soundz, stole a gun, and was devastated by Mario's silence. Are all men awful? What about Drake? I thought he was a good man —kind, thoughtful, getting me the job without expecting anything in return. But is it just an act? Is that how men are in the beginning?

It isn't exactly the first or even *the fifth* time I've been wrong about a man.

Can no-one be trusted? I came to Vegas with a purpose—to reconnect with the New Soundz community and expose Ricky Star for what he is and what he has done—what he's probably still doing. My plan was to make him confess in order to show the world what he's done. At first, I wanted to get justice for Rochelle, but now I know I need to get it for all of his victims. He needs to be fired and exposed. And above all else, to be stopped so that he can't hurt anyone else. But *maybe* that isn't enough.

Lying in bed, I glance down at my phone and open my photos. Here it is—the picture of the gun I swiped from Ricky's office. With trembling fingers, I open a Google image search and upload the photo.

Details about the gun pop up immediately. It's a Smith & Wesson Model 10 that holds six rounds. It's quite popular and costs about a thousand dollars. There are several YouTube videos with demonstrations for cleaning and firing the weapon. *Hmm.*

With knowledge comes power.

I stare at the screen, ideas swirling around of how to use my newfound knowledge.

Would Ricky tell me the truth if I pointed his own gun in his face? Would he admit what he'd done to Rochelle? Would he confess to hurting her—and other women too? Would he finally face justice and rot in prison, where he couldn't hurt anyone ever again?

He needs to pay. Not just for what he did to Rochelle, but for all the others he hurt. For all the women who have been silenced, brutalized, stripped of their power. It's time to take a stand.

Are all men bad, or have I just never met a good one? Maybe Drake is genuine. Or maybe, if I spend more time with him, I'll end up like I did the last time I trusted a man—bruised, battered, and ashamed, lying in a hospital bed.

Never again. I'm not going to lose my power, not this time.

As I drift off to sleep, I think about how Ricky Star stole Rochelle's power, her dignity, and her spark. *I'm going to get it back for you, Rochelle, even if it's the last thing I ever do.*

CHAPTER TWENTY-SEVEN

My second and third days of work were boring and short, with little to do. The New Soundz weren't there and all we did was go over logistics and prepare for Wednesday, when the band would return for another rehearsal. Because of the short shifts, I couldn't risk snooping around the office so soon after Gianni caught me in the hallway. With the plan I have for Ricky, I can't let anything get in my way—like having Gianni become suspicious of me and then fire me.

Thoughts of how I'll take down Ricky run through my mind as I sip my wine and half-listen to Drake talk about his past. Without much else to do, I've spent most of my time plotting and getting to know my new city.

Drake sets his glass down, and says, "We were just kids when we got married. We didn't know much about being adults, and over time, we grew in different directions. There wasn't any infidelity, which is why everyone was so confused when we split up. People couldn't comprehend that after a few years together, we realized we weren't right for each other. We were both better off separate."

His honesty makes me think about my own past. Am I

better off without Joe? *Yes.* I think about how quickly he dumped me to be with his new woman and how he'd explained it wasn't planned but he'd fallen in love with her so fast there was no stopping it. Maybe that was what love was like. There aren't several years of figuring out if you're happy or if your partner is right for you. Maybe I shouldn't be so harsh toward Joe. Him finding someone he *actually* loves and then dumping me might have been the best thing that could've happened. If he hadn't, I would still be his wife, catering to his every whim and living a life of monotony. I just wish he'd never proposed and made me believe I was it for him.

I nod, the thoughts lingering. "I think that's kind of what happened with my ex and me."

Drake looks at me with curiosity. "I'm guessing it was recent?"

"Yeah," I say softly. "The divorce was finalized last week."

"I'm sorry. That's rough."

"I think I'm handling it okay," I say, taking another sip of wine. The warmth of the drink settles my nerves.

"Sounds like you're definitely making a fresh start."

My phone buzzes and I instinctively look at the screen. It's *her* again.

"Do you need to get that?" Drake asks.

"Oh, no. I'm so sorry. I'll put it away." I slip my phone into my purse. It's the third time my therapist's office has tried to call me. I missed my Manic Monday appointment and haven't called to reschedule or cancel. She'll get the message, eventually.

"And yes, I am starting over fresh. And it's been great. Five years ago, if you'd told me I'd be sitting here with you, working on the New Soundz Las Vegas residency, I would've told you you were completely nuts."

Drake chuckles. "Sometimes things happen for a reason. I

don't regret marrying my ex, but I don't regret divorcing her either."

"I completely understand." I raise my glass, grinning. "Here's to mature ways of thinking about our past relationships."

Fake it until you make it? My logical side tells me to think positive about Joe and my split, but the idea of being nice to Joe seems to be too big of an ask at the moment. It's as if my brain has been trained to want to break things when I see his smug face.

We clink glasses and drink. Drake seems genuinely nice. I *want* to trust him, but I don't.

"Gianni says you're doing great at the job," Drake adds after a moment. "Said you work quickly and take direction well."

"I mean, it's not too hard," I say with a shrug. "It's fun—like planning a party. Everything's all set for the dress rehearsal tomorrow night."

"That's great. I think it was a lucky break running into you, especially since we just lost one of our staff."

"Yeah," I say with a nod. "It was meant to be."

"I agree." Drake leans forward slightly. "And during the dress rehearsal tomorrow, you're welcome to sit in the audience."

"Really?"

"We're inviting a few small groups for it. Kind of like a soft launch, just to get some feedback. Insiders only. It'll give the performers a sense of having an audience."

I'm a New Soundz insider. Did you hear that, Rochelle? "How many rehearsals will there be?"

"There will be three more after tomorrow's. They want everything perfect for every show in the residency. We'll be crossing every 'T' and dotting every 'I' until the last second.

We'll do the final sound check the morning of the first show. It's a lot of work for everyone," he says. "I'm glad you're here."

His words feel sincere, and I can't help but feel like maybe he isn't terrible. *Time will tell.*

"Me too."

When the check comes, Drake reaches for it, but I stop him. "Oh no, I'm taking you out. You've given me a job *and* fulfilled a childhood dream of meeting the New Soundz. I'm taking care of this," I insist, placing my card onto the billfold.

"Okay, okay," he says with a good-natured smile, raising his hands in mock surrender.

There is nothing about him that makes me think he is dangerous; there is nothing to suggest he could be like Ricky or Sam or the others who hurt women. But then again, there were no warnings about the others either. Is it a problem that I am starting to feel a little attracted to him? I hope it won't cloud my judgement. First and foremost, I need to take down Ricky.

After paying the bill, Drake offers to walk me back to my hotel. I accept, feeling a flutter of anticipation. This is the ultimate test—to see if he is like the others or if he truly is a gentleman. Is it worth the risk?

As we stroll, he asks, "How long do you plan to stay at the hotel?"

"At least a month. It's not bad, actually. I kind of like it. I'm right in the middle of everything—I can walk everywhere. Plus, I'm starting to figure out the bus lines. I was even thinking about visiting the Grand Canyon."

"It's really spectacular."

"And the Hoover Dam. They both seem so interesting. I've only seen them in movies, never in person."

"Well, if you want to do a day trip, I'd be happy to take you," Drake offers. "The West Rim is only about two hours from here, and the Hoover Dam is just thirty minutes away."

"That would be awesome."

By the time we reach the lobby of my hotel, I have made my decision. I think I can trust him or at least test to see if I can. He's been nothing but kind and respectful all evening. Surely, if he were the type to hurt me, he wouldn't be suggesting road trips or walking me back like this. Still, there is a sliver of doubt.

I stop just before the elevators and turn to him. "Do you want to come up for a drink? I've got a somewhat stocked kitchen," I say with a playful smile. Thankfully there is a Target store just around the corner from my hotel where I'm able to buy basic groceries.

Drake hesitates briefly, then says, "I'd like that."

My pulse races as I lead him to my suite. Inside, I gesture around the space. "This is it," I say, trying to keep the mood light. "I've got a kitchen, living room, bedroom, a nice-sized bathroom, and even a washer and dryer. I'm all set." I grin and walk to the windows, pulling back the shades to reveal the glittering Las Vegas Strip. "And the view isn't bad either."

Drake steps closer, taking in the scene. "I admit, it's pretty cool. I can see why you want to stay here."

For a moment, we stand in silence, admiring the city lights, and I feel a flicker of hope—maybe, just maybe, I can trust him.

"I really do," I say with a smile, turning back toward the kitchen. "I've got a bottle of red open—want some?"

He smiles. "Sure."

I pull down two glasses from the cupboard and pour, not quite to the brim, but a generous amount. With both glasses clutched carefully in my hands, I walk over to the table and hand him one.

We clink glasses, the soft ting breaking the quiet of the room. We move to the sofa and sit down. I kick off my shoes and tuck my legs as he settles in beside me.

"Do you date much?"

"Not too much," he says, a faint blush rising to his cheeks. Is he nervous too? "What about you?" he asks, turning the question back to me. "Have you dated much since the divorce?"

I study my wine, considering how to answer. "Just a little here and there. Nothing serious. I just want to have fun for a little while. I feel like I'm starting my life all over again, and so far, it's been pretty great." *Not all of it, but some of it.*

"That's good."

I set my glass down on the table and, without thinking too much, place my hand on his thigh. He freezes for a moment and then turns to look at me, his eyes searching mine. Slowly, he sets his glass down and cups my cheeks with his hands, pulling me into a kiss. It's warm, tender, and unhurried—so unlike the rushed and rough encounters I've had recently. Maybe I can trust him.

I WAKE the next morning with a smile on my face, memories of the night washing over me. It had been one of the most intimate, exhilarating experiences of my life. *Quite surprising.* I stretch, reaching for him in bed, but my hand finds only the sheets.

Sitting up, I listen for any signs of him—footsteps in the kitchen, the sound of the shower—but there is nothing. I climb out of bed, the good mood slipping away as I hurry around the hotel suite.

He isn't here.

He's gone.

Panic sets in as my mind jumps to the worst possible thought. Did he see the gun? Heart pounding, I rush to the nightstand and yank open the drawer. I pull out the towel and relief rushes through me when I see it's still there. But that doesn't mean he didn't see it. It just means he didn't take it. Do I need to worry?

I let out a shaky breath and turn my attention to my phone on the nightstand. A notification blinks on the screen. It's a text from Drake.

> Had a great time last night. See you at work.

I stare at the message, my emotions tangled. Why did he leave without saying anything? Is that strange, or is that just how things are? Did he think it was a casual one-night stand? My mind goes dark, and I run into the bathroom and stare in the mirror. I'm stark naked, but as I search for signs of abuse, there are none. The memories of pleasure and no pain are real. Does that mean I can trust him or only that I can trust him to not drug and beat me?

Rochelle, what do you think? Should I go for him, for real? Maybe after I get what I need from him?

Sitting all alone, I realize I like his company. His touch. It feels good to feel wanted. Maybe I don't want it to be just a means to an end with him. And it hits me like a lightning bolt. For the first time in a long time, I *really* want someone—and I want that someone to want me just as bad. I smack my cheek and stare in the mirror. I say, "No, Jess. Stay focused. You have work to do."

CHAPTER TWENTY-EIGHT

My body is buzzing. Not only am I about to see Drake but it's also the dress rehearsal for the New Soundz residency. I can't wait to listen, to be transported back to a time when everything else stood still. Back when nothing else mattered.

When all my problems vanished—the nights when Mom was too drunk to sign permission forms, running out of toilet paper and having to use napkins I'd picked up from McDonald's after school. It's funny how I didn't think about those things until now. These memories were covered up with my determination to have a better life than the one I came from.

Knowing I didn't have anyone looking out for me, I had to grow up fast. There wasn't someone worried if I had food for lunch or a way to get to school. I babysat for neighbors and saved all I had for essentials like food. Bagels were always a favorite because they were cheap, and they filled me up. Pizza was a second favorite since you could get two pizzas for a deal.

It's sort of funny how in adulthood I'd practically shunned carbs most of the time. I thought it was about losing weight, about being thin, about being what Joe wanted me to be. But maybe it was more than that. Maybe I just didn't want anything to do with my childhood—a childhood that included bagels, cheap pizza, and endless survival strategies. Sometimes, I wonder how I even made it through those years. I think it was because of my little sister.

She was so innocent, so hopeful. She made me believe that things could be different, that we could start fresh. Unfortunately, she fell into the ways of my mother by the time puberty hit. It nearly broke my heart. But that didn't stop me from believing I could be something different. I always had hope. Maybe that was how I'd escaped being just a data point on the endless cycle.

That hope and confidence will serve me well in my new life, one I hope includes Drake when all of this is over. If not Drake, someone like him. Considering he may never talk to me again if he learns my true intentions.

With a quick rap on his open door, I catch his attention. He moves his gaze from his computer monitor to me. His smile is immediate. Definitely a good sign. I walk in and gently close the door behind me.

"Hi, Jess."

"Hi," I say, trying to steady the excitement in my voice. "I had a really good time last night. But I was surprised to wake up and you weren't there."

"I had an early meeting," he says. "I needed time to get home, shower, and change. I'm sorry—was that rude? I don't do this much. I'm not sure of the protocol." His eyes search mine, filled with genuine concern.

"I don't either. It's totally fine," I say quickly. "I was just a little worried. I wanted to make sure everything was okay."

"Yeah, totally."

"Is it something you'd like to do again?" I ask. "Maybe not tonight, because I think we'll be here late, but maybe tomorrow night?"

The dress rehearsal starts at six PM and then there is clean up. I don't want to push too hard or overwhelm him. I want to keep things relaxed. I want to enjoy him, savor him, like a fine wine—all while getting closer to my target.

"I'd like that."

"Great," I say, feeling a wave of triumph.

He stands up, walking around the desk until he's right in front of me. He says, "Is it okay if I kiss you? I didn't get to kiss you goodbye this morning. Would that be okay?"

I nod eagerly, unable to stop the wide smile spreading across my face. I probably look like a complete goon, but I don't care. He leans in, and when his lips meet mine, my whole body tingles. The electricity is undeniable, and from the way he lingers, I know he feels it too. And I think, of course I can have Drake and complete my mission. It's not one or the other. Like how I'm able to move forward with my plan to destroy Ricky while being a part of the New Soundz community. It's not a matter of one or the other. I can have it all. *Don't you think so, Rochelle?*

"That was good," he murmurs, pulling back slightly. "But we probably shouldn't do too much of this here at work."

I nod while trying to look composed. "Of course not. I have to meet Gianni. I'll see you later."

"See you later."

I slip out of his office, feeling lighter than I have in years. He feels it too—I can tell. I believe Drake and I can be happy together. But even in this moment of elation, my mind spins with a darker thought. He can't know about my plans for Ricky because he may try to stop me, and I can't let that happen. *I have to destroy him, by any means necessary.*

CHAPTER TWENTY-NINE

STANDING IN THE FRONT ROW, my adrenaline is in overdrive as I wait for the New Soundz to take the stage. The lights blast and the band ascends. I have never been this close before—front-row seats were always out of reach. Back then, we couldn't get them, no matter how hard we tried. Even after spending two nights in line with Rochelle and her mom, hoping to snag primo tickets, the best we got was seventh row. The floor seats were awesome, but they weren't *front row*.

Even though we didn't get the absolute best tickets, our campout for tickets was an event in itself. In preparation, we packed a suitcase full of snacks, sodas, clean clothes, and blankets. I think back to those memories of Rochelle and her mom, how we giggled, told stories, and ate candy to pass the time. I'd give anything to relive those moments—sleeping bags wrapped around us, huddled close, drinking soda and sharing snacks. We barely slept, but that didn't matter. As soon as the store lights flicked on and the front doors cracked open, the excitement was unbearable. The clerk stepped out and called out, "It's time!" and we jumped up, screeching the way only teenage girls do when they're about to buy concert tickets for their favorite band. The campouts were almost as fun as the concerts themselves.

All these years later, standing in the front row, I still wish Rochelle was next to me. Would she still love them after all these years too? Would she still believe in this magic, like we once did?

After what happened with Ricky, Rochelle withdrew into herself. Her letters to me grew more depressing, lacking the bubbly doodles and cheery scribbles she used to include in the margins. She used to sign every letter with some variation of "Ethan and Rochelle forever." Ethan was her favorite band member, and she always said she'd grow up to marry him. But as time went on, the Rochelle I knew began to fade. Her light dimmed, and her words grew darker. It wasn't fair what he did to her.

Alex greets the small crowd. "Hello, Las Vegas! How are you feeling tonight?"

My mind shoots back to the moment, to the now, and I scream my reply—not just for me, but for Rochelle too.

As the band introduces themselves and converses with the crowd, I lose myself in their magnetism. The stage bursts with a light show, and Ethan opens the set with one of my favorites. I sing along and dance as if I am transported to another space and time, and in my mind, she's with me, and I say, "Can you believe it? We're really here!"

The few dozen people in the audience are on their feet too, singing and cheering them on. I surmise most of them are probably industry professionals, family, friends, and special VIPs. And me. Being included is unfathomable.

The air is electric.

The smiles from the guys, the way they look at me, as if they are singing right to me. Even now, staring at their forty-something-year-old selves—they make me feel the magic again. After all the years, all I've lived, and all I've endured, they still have that power over me.

Someone touches my arm, and for just a fleeting second, I think it's Rochelle. My heart leaps before reality hits me. It isn't her—it's Drake.

"They're incredible," I say, leaning close so he can hear me over the music. "Just like twenty years ago. Maybe even better."

"I'm glad you're enjoying the show," he says with a smile as he stands next to me, watching the concert. The entire set is nearly three hours. Three hours of joy tinged with a few fleeting moments of deep sadness and regret.

It's nice to have Drake to share the concert with, but it isn't the same as if it were Rochelle. It will never be exactly the way it was. It's wonderful, but it will never be the pure bliss it once was. The memories of before are kept locked away in a place only I can reach. I can't let it pull me down. *I have to make new memories, and I will.*

The audience erupts into cheers, pulling me back in once again. Drake turns to me, flashing a smile. "Awesome show! They're going to kill it!"

"Yes. They're incredible."

"I have to meet with some folks backstage. I'll call you tomorrow?"

I nod, smiling back, and watch Drake walk away before hurrying back to my catering station. The people who have come in for the dress rehearsal will be eating soon, and I need to make sure everything is set—food, beverages, all of it. Although my position doesn't require a fancy college degree or come with a six-figure salary, it is by far the best job I've ever had. It doesn't pay much, and I am still mostly living off my savings, but it doesn't matter. I wouldn't trade this experience for anything.

Before the audience floods the catering area, I spot the band coming off the stage. They are drenched in sweat, smiles stretched across their faces, still glowing from their performance. My heart races as I hurry up to them.

"You guys were incredible!"

Ethan grins at me. "Thank you so much, Jess!"

He remembers my name. I am screaming on the inside like a teenage girl at my first concert. The others chime in with their thanks as well, *except for Mario*. He only gives me a brief glance, but his eyes linger on mine for a moment too long, and I see something there. It's like he doesn't want to see me, doesn't want to talk to me. He probably wishes I weren't there—that I didn't know his secret.

As they head toward their dressing rooms, I call out, "Let me know if you need anything. You too, *Mario*."

Mario doesn't respond. He just looks back at me once more before following the others. The catering area is starting to fill up, and I have to abandon my mission for now. But we will meet later, and when we do, I will get the answers I need. *I am not done with you, Mario—not yet.*

CHAPTER THIRTY

AFTER A LONG NIGHT of small talk and fetching drinks, I start to clean up the mess. Drake wasn't kidding when he said it would be exhausting, but it still feels more like a party than work. Working with the New Soundz is like that; every day is a celebration.

Most of the band has stopped by the catering table for snacks and a chat during the evening—except Mario. He is noticeably absent, and I can't shake the feeling that he is avoiding me. Ricky hasn't shown up either, which isn't unusual, but it gnaws at me. Where is he?

Gianni has gone out to meet with vendors, leaving the backstage area quieter than usual. I decide it's the perfect moment to take my chance. Mario's dressing room is down the hall. My heart pounds as I approach the door, finding it closed. I knock twice, the sound echoing in the empty corridor. No response.

Glancing around to make sure no one is watching, I take a deep breath and turn the handle. The door creaks as I push it open. Mario is sitting on a couch on the right side of the room. His posture is slouched, his head leaning back against the cushions, but the moment he sees me, his eyes lock onto mine.

"What are you doing in here?" His tone is sharp and his brow furrowed in annoyance.

I step inside, shutting the door behind me. "Mario, I need your help."

"You're not supposed to be in here," he says, sitting up straighter. "I want you to leave."

"Please." My voice trembles. "I'm begging you."

He sighs, his shoulders sagging in defeat. "What do you need?"

"First of all, you guys were incredible out there. I really appreciate being here. I'm a huge fan—I always have been, and I always will be."

Without emotion, he says, "Thanks."

I know he is good on the inside. I know he'll help me if I can just get him to listen. I swallow hard, willing myself to speak the words that have been lodged in my throat for days.

"Mario, when I was fifteen, my friend Rochelle and I went to all your concerts. It was everything to us. At our fourth concert, we stuck around after the show, trying to get close to the stage…"

I tell him everything—everything that happened that night. My voice shakes as I speak, the words pouring out in a flood I can't stop. Mario's expression darkens with every detail. When I finish, he shuts his eyes and places his head in his hands.

"I have a feeling," I say softly, "by the look on your face and your reaction, that she wasn't his only victim."

He rakes his fingers through his hair, his jaw tight. When he finally meets my gaze, his eyes are filled with something new—regret, anger, maybe both.

"No," he says.

"Why?" I ask. "Why would you keep his secret? How many others are there?"

Mario sighs heavily, running a hand through his hair. "I

don't know how many there were, but I caught Ricky once with a young girl and confronted him. I told him I would expose him."

"Why didn't you?"

I wish I had been recording the conversation because I need something concrete, something I can use against Ricky. But at least I have Mario talking now.

"You seem like such a good guy," I say. "Why didn't you say something?"

Mario looks down, his expression clouded with guilt. "It was different back then. I was a gay man in a boy band. Our manager controlled everything we said, what we wore, and where we were allowed to be. He controlled *everything* in our lives. It wasn't like it is now. Our manager and my agent told me to make sure no one ever knew I was gay. We were supposed to be male heartthrobs who wanted and needed attention from teenage girls. They were the demographic our managers were after. Being a gay man wasn't the right image. They told me it would ruin *all* of our careers."

My chest tightens as I listen. "Ricky knew you were gay?"

He nods, his voice quieter now. "Yeah, he knew."

I soften my tone. "I think it's great that you came out. And if it makes you feel any better, I would've still loved you back then, even if I knew you were gay."

He smiles faintly, but it doesn't reach his eyes. "Thanks. But you don't represent everybody. Back then, it felt like it could be the end of the world if anyone found out. It ate me up inside. When I confronted Ricky, he threatened me. Told me he'd ruin my career—and the rest of the New Soundz too."

"I guess I can see why you kept quiet," I say. "But times have changed. Look at what's happened in the last five, ten years. With the #MeToo movement, these things are finally coming to light. Why don't you come forward now? Why not tell someone about Ricky?"

"I don't have any proof," he says. "It's just my word against his."

"Maybe if you'd said something—made an allegation—other women would've felt empowered to come forward. They might have seen you as someone who believed them, someone who could stand with them. It would give them courage to tell their story."

"I should have," he says. "But Ricky is powerful. He told me he'd ruin me, and I believed him. I was just a kid back then. Now, it's not just about me anymore. I'm married. We have a child. I can't let anything happen to them."

I can see the pain he carries, the years of guilt and fear that have shaped his decisions. But it isn't enough—not for Rochelle, not for the others Ricky has hurt.

And certainly not for me.

Ricky has put Mario in a terrible position. "What if we expose him together?" I ask, desperate to find some way to make him see the importance of this.

Mario shakes his head firmly. "Look, I'm sorry, but I can't. I really can't risk it, and I can't let you do it either. If you expose him, he'll think it was me. I just can't let you do it."

I stare at him, disbelief washing over me.

Shrugging, he adds, "I don't know. I just... I need you to promise me you won't go forward with this. You need to let it go."

"Let it go?" I say, my voice rising. "I can't. It's part of my plan."

"Your plan?" he asks, narrowing his eyes.

"That incident—it's why Rochelle and I stopped going to your concerts. We lost something so major that day, Mario. We lost a huge part of our lives, part of who we were. I'm trying to get it back, but I can't until I right that wrong."

Mario's face twists with anguish. "I'm sorry, Jess. Please don't. I've already said too much. I need you to leave."

He is clearly tortured by this, and part of me understands. But another part can't let it go. With a quick nod, I step toward the door, my hand resting on the cool metal knob. Before turning it, I look back at him and say, "This isn't over, Mario."

I leave the room without another word, my nerves rattling. As the door clicks shut behind me, I think to myself, *Far from over, Mario.*

The hallway feels stifling, and I take a deep breath to steady my nerves. I barely have time to process what just happened when I nearly run smack into Gianni, who seemingly appears out of nowhere. "What were you doing in there, Jess?"

CHAPTER THIRTY-ONE

Gianni glares at me. "Why was the door closed?"

I quickly respond, "Mario needed something, so I went in and gave it to him."

He crosses his arms, his glare unwavering. "Why was the door closed?" he demands again.

"It was a sensitive matter," I say, thinking quickly on my feet.

"Like what?"

"He needed water, and I noticed he seemed a little upset. I asked him what was wrong, and I figured he might need some privacy, so I closed the door. It's not a big deal."

"So, Mario is confiding in you these days?"

I shrug, trying to appear casual. "Honestly, I think it was just one of those right-place, right-time moments. He said he was feeling old—you know, being in his late-forties and still dancing around on stage. He says it's exhilarating but sometimes it takes a toll. It's not a big deal."

"Okay," Gianni says at last, though his tone suggests he isn't entirely convinced. He doesn't seem satisfied with my explanation but doesn't press further.

I take a breath, relieved to steer the conversation to an end. "Anything else I can do for you tonight?"

"No, I think we're just about done here. Have a good night."

"I will. You too," I say in a chipper tone, hurrying toward the exit.

But the truth is, I will have a good evening because I have a plan. If Mario won't help me, I have to find another way to expose Ricky—for everything. Surely, there has to be a record somewhere. Lawsuits, documents, anything that gives even a hint of suspicion. If something exists, I will find it. But I know I have to tread carefully. I don't want Mario to get in trouble, especially since he has already covered for Ricky all these years. Part of me understands why he has. He's been stuck in a situation that could have destroyed not only his life and career but the rest of the New Soundz too. And I don't want them destroyed any more than Mario does. *See, Rochelle, he is a good guy!*

I cross the cool Vegas Strip, the twinkling lights stretching across the skyline, and make my way across the sky bridge back to my hotel. The thought strikes me—I would have fallen apart if the New Soundz had been ruined by a scandal. *I have to protect them.* Like Rochelle, they deserve justice too.

Now, I can see it clearly. Mario is a victim, just like Rochelle. He's been blackmailed all these years, and I have to expose Ricky for all his awful deeds. But I don't want Mario—or the rest of the New Soundz—to look bad. They aren't guilty. They don't deserve the fallout. Ricky is the monster, not them.

Rochelle deserves justice, and so do the others Ricky has hurt. If the New Soundz and Ricky never know it was me who exposes Ricky, who brings his darkness to an end, that's okay. That's what you do for the people you love. You put yourself aside and don't seek recognition or gratitude; you do it because you want their lives to be better. Because you want them to be happy.

I pass a group of drunken tourists stumbling down the steps and think for a moment, *Is this selfish?* Maybe a little, but deep down, I truly want what is best for all of them. And this—this is what is best. I couldn't protect Rochelle—or Mario—all those years ago, but I can and *will* do it now.

CHAPTER THIRTY-TWO

AFTER A DECADENT STEAK dinner with Drake, we stroll hand-in-hand back to my hotel room. Everything feels easy with him. Drake is kind and sweet, grounded in a way that makes me feel safe. He doesn't sigh when I order the beef Wellington or a second glass of wine or dessert. He isn't full of himself, never boasting about his accomplishments or his past. He isn't like Joe. Drake is a real man, the kind of person who deserves love and all the good things life has to offer.

He is, in some ways, like Rochelle. She never judged or bragged about all the things her parents gave her. She was down to earth and an all-around lovely person. Rochelle's face flashes in my mind, followed by the guilt of how I couldn't save her. I know it isn't totally rational. I was just a child then. But still, I knew she was struggling after the attack. When Rochelle withdrew from everything and everyone, including me, I should have pushed harder.

She stopped wanting to talk on the phone, and I gave up after trying a hundred times to get her to pick up. Her letters became sad and lifeless. She wrote about how she didn't have the energy to do much of anything, but that didn't matter too much because she never felt like doing anything anyway. She stopped visiting with her other friends and spent most of her time alone in her room reading or sleeping. Her grades slipped to the point where she was barely passing her classes. Her parents thought she was on drugs—but I knew she wasn't. The letters, once a constant, became fewer and fewer. Weekly turned into biweekly, then monthly.

Eventually, her parents became so desperate they transferred her to private school and sent her to a doctor and then to a psychiatrist. But from what little Rochelle shared in her letters, it was clear none of it was helping. As an adult, I now understand that she was suffering from depression. Dangerously so. I wish I'd understood back then. All I knew at the time was that she was slipping further and further away from me and everyone else.

My rational brain thinks there wasn't a whole lot more I could have done. It's not like I had a cell phone back then or a way to reach her parents directly. I couldn't drive and didn't have money for the bus and train. And since Rochelle didn't want to see me, her mom stopped picking me up like she used to. Bit by bit, Rochelle faded away, and it nearly broke me.

Drake says, "Did you have fun tonight?"

I barely hear him, still lost in my thoughts. Rochelle's memory weighs heavily, as if it has suddenly crawled out from the back of my mind to haunt me daily and in my dreams. It's likely the nightmares won't stop until I make things right.

"Are you okay?" he asks.

I glance over at him, shaking off the melancholy. "Yeah, I'm fine. Just... old memories."

"Do you want to talk about it?"

I reach up and trace my finger along his cheek, marveling at how sweet and caring he is. "Not tonight, but thank you. I appreciate it."

He nods, but before we step through the entrance of the hotel, I pause. "Do you want to come up?"

A smile spreads across his face. "Sure, if you're up for it."

"I am," I say softly. "I want to spend time with you." I like having him around, even if I don't want to talk. It's nice to not be alone even if it's just for a little while.

We enter through the automatic doors and step into the elevator, still hand in hand. I try not to let myself think about this relationship beyond my plans for Ricky. I know it might not end well for us. Drake is sweet but maybe not able to understand why what I have to do is so important. And it's most likely that when he learns the truth, he may hate me. It's a risk I have to take.

Once inside my hotel room, Drake makes himself comfortable on the sofa while I pour us some wine in the kitchenette. It's nice, almost domestic in its simplicity. This is only our second real date, but I enjoy my time with him. Everything is falling into place, going according to plan. And now, I have a new improved plan—one I believe in.

With the wine glasses in hand, I set aside my laptop to place them in front of Drake. The glow of the screen catches his attention, and he does a double take.

"Why are you reading about Ricky Star on the internet?"

Panic surges through me. What will he think if he knows I'm digging into Ricky's background? Will he think I'm stalking him—or worse? He can't know what I'm up to.

I scramble for a response. "Oh, I was just looking up his history. I know he was the tour manager back when the New Soundz toured before." I quickly shut the laptop lid and sit down beside Drake, trying to play it off. Taking a gulp of wine—definitely not very ladylike—I place my hand on his thigh and lean in to kiss him. The warmth of his lips distracts me, if only for a moment, from the tension in my chest. Hopefully, it will distract him too.

What he's seen on my computer isn't exactly damning, but it isn't innocent either. I'm not stalking Ricky—I'm investigating him. Gathering evidence. Doing what I need to do to expose him for the predator he is. What I have uncovered so far is as bad as Mario has alluded to. Three lawsuits, all settled out of court, with the details sealed. No victims' names and no settlement amounts. All I can piece together is that the cases date back to the late '90s.

Ricky might have flown under the radar back then because he wasn't a big name yet. Maybe the women were too scared to come forward. But now? Now, if I launch a campaign—if I do it the right way—I bet other victims will step out of the shadows. Older and wiser now, they will be confident enough to expose him for the piece of garbage he's always been.

I let myself melt into Drake's warm embrace, savoring the comfort and safety of the moment. But deep down, I know I can't stay here forever. If Ricky somehow retaliates, if he blackmails or threatens anyone again, I can't allow it. I have to protect Drake, the New Soundz, and any woman who might still be vulnerable to Ricky's predation.

And I know exactly what I'm going to do to expose him. There won't be any more victims. *Not on my watch.*

CHAPTER THIRTY-THREE

A WEEK LATER, I stand backstage, full of confidence. The moment I've been preparing for is upon me. After the rehearsal, I'm going to corner Ricky and get him to talk about the "old days," bait him into self-incrimination. My goal is to gather soundbites of him saying something damning and something disgusting that I can use for my campaign to expose him. Surely, that tiger hasn't changed his stripes.

The plan is simple: get close to Ricky, make him think I'm on his side. Befriend him, offer him drinks, and coax him into lowering his guard. It will be the perfect addition to the plan I've meticulously mapped out. I've already bought a small recorder, the kind that can run discreetly without him ever knowing. It doesn't need to be admissible in court—it just needs to work for social media, for the victims. The women need to know he's still out there, still dangerous. Together we can destroy him.

I'm not exactly sure how I'll get him to open up, but I have to trust my instincts. Men like Ricky are arrogant; they believe they're untouchable. That arrogance will be his downfall.

As I make my final preparations for the evening, Gianni approaches me. "Hey, Jess, how's it going?"

"Great! Looks like we've got everything set for today. Is there anything else you need?" I say, keeping my tone cheerful.

"Not much," Gianni says with a grin. "Just wait for the crew to come in, and we'll get ready for another rehearsal. You saw how it went last time—we've got about the same number of people coming tonight. They'll need help with cleanup—you know the drill. You're a quick learner."

"Thank you so much! I try my best," I say with a smile, relieved to see that Gianni isn't holding a grudge from his suspicions about me outside Mario's dressing room last week. Since then, I've backed off of Mario and set my sights on figuring out how to expose Ricky.

I continue organizing backstage, running through my mental checklist. Just then, I hear voices—Mario and Ethan. I glance over and wave. "Hi, Ethan! Hi, Mario!"

Ethan smiles warmly. "Hey, Jess."

Mario, on the other hand, mumbles a halfhearted, "Hi," in a low voice.

I sigh internally. *Geez, could he at least pretend to be friendly?* Still, I believe he'll come around, eventually. Someday, after I expose Ricky, Mario will be free of the secrets, the blackmail, and the crushing pressure he's been living under. He'll thank me later.

For a moment, I stop to take it all in. How did I get here? How did I end up working backstage with Ethan and Mario from the New Soundz? They know *my name*. It's been just under two weeks since I moved to Vegas, met Drake, and started working with the crew. It all still feels surreal, like the last twenty years have been a dull, gray painting. Now, everything is bursting with color, glitz, and glamor—just like Las Vegas itself.

And just as if the universe has been reading my thoughts,

Ricky walks in, and right into my trap. "Hey, Ricky! How are you doing today? Can I get you anything?" I ask sweetly, keeping my tone light and friendly.

Ricky's eyes land on me, lingering a second too long. He gives me that familiar smirk, the kind that makes my stomach churn. He isn't subtle in his appraisal—not that I'm some fresh-faced, wide-eyed fifteen-year-old anymore. But I still have my assets, and I can tell he appreciates them. "No, thanks."

This is my chance. I smile warmly, suppressing the bile rising in my throat. *The game has begun.* "Okay. I'll stop by your office later to see if you need anything."

"All right. See you later," Ricky says before walking out.

I watch him go, resisting the urge to roll my eyes. Clearly, I'm not his type—perhaps about twenty years too old for the creep.

With a sigh, I turn back to fussing over the catering setup. The first round of snacks has just arrived, and I want everything to look perfect. I begin arranging the platters neatly on the table, making sure every detail is just right. Grabbing a pretzel, I pop it into my mouth—salty, crunchy, and delicious.

Footsteps approach from behind, and I glance over my shoulder. A wide grin spreads across my face. "Hi, Drake."

"Hey, I just wanted to come by and say hi before the show starts."

I smile, stepping closer to him. My hand instinctively goes to his hip, and I lean in for a kiss—but stop myself at the last moment. "Oh, we probably shouldn't do that here, huh?" I whisper.

"Probably not," he says, though his smile tells me he doesn't mind.

I love it—this feeling, this connection with him. We've gone out a few times this past week, and it's already one of the best relationships I've been in. For once, everything seems to be going right. It's so empowering, almost euphoric. I want to shout from the rooftops, "Life can be amazing if you just believe in yourself. Follow your passions, trust your instincts, and do what's right—everything good will come to you!"

But the moment doesn't last.

Footsteps pound toward us, and we step apart just as Ricky storms in. He faces Drake and says, "I need to talk to you privately."

Drake looks surprised but nods.

"My office," Ricky commands, gesturing toward the back. The two of them hurry off, leaving me standing there, puzzled.

What is that about? Something about Ricky's tone doesn't sit right. Part of me wants to sneak closer, to eavesdrop, but I can't risk it. Everything is going too well—I can't afford to get caught.

A few minutes later, Gianni rushes past, looking flustered. "Everything okay?" I call out.

"Got a bit of a situation. Just keep doing what you're doing. I'll talk to you later," he says as he hurries down the hall toward Ricky's office.

Panic fills me. *What is going on?*

CHAPTER THIRTY-FOUR

Members of the crew are rushing back and forth with upset, serious faces, and I can't shake the feeling that something big has happened. Curiosity gets the better of me, and when the coast is clear, I tiptoe down the hall toward Ricky's office.

Standing in the hallway, I strain to hear the voices through the closed door. Raised voices, definitely, but the words are muffled. My recorder won't help me. As I edge closer, I suddenly hear footsteps approaching from the other side. My heart skips a beat. Panicked, I rush back down the hallway, heading backstage where I'm supposed to be.

I busy myself, setting things on the table just right, arranging snacks, and double-checking every detail. Still, my thoughts race. What happened? Why does everyone look so freaked out?

Moments later, all three men—Drake, Ricky, and Gianni—come charging toward me. My heart pounds, doubling, tripling in speed. Drake's eyes lock on mine. "Stay here. We need to have a quick meeting with everyone on-site, okay?"

"Sure, of course," I say, trying to keep my voice steady.

Something is wrong—terribly wrong. Fear seeps inside me. What if something happened to one of the New Soundz? The thought makes my stomach clench. If one of them got hurt... That would be awful—devastating.

Soon, the crew gathers near the seating area. Drake motions for me to join the group. I glance around, counting heads. The electricians, the sound crew... the New Soundz. One, two, three, four, five—they're all there. Relief washes over me. At least they're okay. But what could this be about?

Drake steps forward, his expression grim. "We have a bit of a situation."

The crew exchanges murmurs, whispers of speculation rippling through the group. Is it something related to the show? A technical issue?

Drake raises a hand, silencing the chatter. "Ricky recently discovered that something is missing from his office. It's... sensitive in nature."

Sensitive? My breath hitches as realization dawns. The gun. He's realized the gun is missing. *Oh, no, Rochelle. What if they know I took it?*

One of the electricians—Donald I think his name is—speaks up. "What is it? What's missing?"

Drake's gaze sweeps over the entire group, landing on each person in turn, including me. His voice is low but firm. "Ricky had a firearm in his desk. It's gone."

Gasps and startled whispers erupt from the crew. Drake continues, his tone sharp. "As you can imagine, this is very serious. If someone took something as dangerous as that, they could have nefarious intentions. I'll be speaking with each of you individually to see if you saw or heard anything. This won't be taken lightly."

Nods of agreement ripple through the group. Some crew members exchange bewildered glances, as though they can't believe there was a gun in Ricky Star's office in the first place. I certainly hadn't expected it when I found it and *took it*.

My palms grow clammy as Drake's piercing eyes scan the crowd again. I stand as still as I can, determined not to draw any suspicion. I fight to maintain a neutral expression as my mind spins. What possessed me to take it? I don't even have a plan for it. All I know is that I can't confess. Nobody can ever know. Should I get rid of it? But how?

CHAPTER THIRTY-FIVE

Everyone in the auditorium has been interviewed by Drake and Gianni to learn if they've seen anyone going in or out of Ricky's office, if anyone has looked out of place, or if we know anything about the missing gun. I kept my answers calm and convincing. They don't seem suspicious of me at all. That's the good news. The bad news is that due to the possible threat to the New Soundz and the crew, the rehearsal is postponed. I didn't expect that, and I hope it won't jeopardize the first show of the residency. Management is being very cautious and is bringing in a security crew to check the venue for any and all threats before the band takes the stage again. I was grateful they put the safety of the New Soundz above all else, but it was bad news for me and the mission.

After being excused, I pack up my bag for the night, relieved the questioning is finally over. Still, as I zip my bag, I can't shake the thought, *I have to get rid of it.* The gun is too dangerous to keep around, especially with Drake coming over more often. The last thing I need is for him to stumble upon it. If I'm smart, I'll take care of it soon.

I've heard that Lake Mead is a well-known local dump site

not far from the Strip, where all kinds of unsavory items are discarded and later found—dead bodies (likely mob hits) and plenty of weapons. Another gun tossed there wouldn't raise any alarms or lead back to me. Maybe I could rent a car, take it out there under the guise of sightseeing. Or... I could make it a date with Drake. Bring the gun along, hidden in my bag, and casually dispose of it when he isn't looking. *No.* Too risky.

Lost in my thoughts, I don't hear anyone approach. I jump slightly when I look up and see Mario standing in front of me.

"How are you?" he asks.

"I'm fine. Thanks," I say, trying to mask my surprise.

He hesitates, his eyes narrowing. "Was it you?"

I blink, playing dumb. "Was what me?"

"Did you take Ricky's gun?"

"Of course not. Don't be ridiculous."

"Well, if anyone around here has a reason to go after Ricky, it's you."

I freeze. He's accusing me outright, and I can't believe it. But I don't hold it against him. He isn't wrong—I do have reasons to despise Ricky. I don't like the way he *assaults* women. That isn't just a pet peeve of mine. It's my driving motivation. "It's not me, Mario. Trust me," I say and then try to assure him. "Look, I'm not going to tell anyone what you told me before. Don't worry."

"But... You're not going to let this go, are you?"

I meet his gaze. "What do you mean?"

"What we talked about before. Keeping quiet. Letting it go."

"I promise none of this will get back to you."

He takes a step closer, lowering his voice. "What are you planning?"

"Don't worry about it. But you're right. This isn't over. I can't just stand by and let Ricky get away with everything he's done. I've looked him up. He's had multiple complaints, settled lawsuits for undisclosed amounts to unnamed victims. He has to be stopped. But," I add firmly, "I didn't take his gun."

"Be careful, Jess," he says softly. "This could end badly."

With that, Mario turns and leaves as quickly as he appeared.

The conversation was short but intense, leaving my mind reeling. I stand there for a moment, still clutching my bag, trying to process what just happened. I had a private conversation with Mario from the New Soundz. Him and me—bonded by a shared secret.

I can't help but think that Mario will thank me when this is all over. Maybe we'll even become good friends, and he'll invite me to his home for BBQs, and I'll get to know his husband and child. We could double date. *Wouldn't that be something, Rochelle?* It's also possible he'll hate me. I can't worry about that at the moment—I have work to do.

CHAPTER THIRTY-SIX

Hunched over my laptop, I begin researching different ways to get to Lake Mead. There are tours, and there are rental cars. Maybe a tour would be best, unless they check bags for bombs or weapons before getting on the bus. A romantic outing with Drake could work if I'm really careful. There will need to be a distraction of some kind so I can carefully toss the gun into the lake. Should I try to file off the serial number first? Is that even something you can do?

I vaguely recall a Forensic Files episode I watched late one night when I couldn't sleep. They mentioned that even if you file off the serial number, the imprint can still be detected in the metal underneath. It's embedded lower and lower into the gun. Would that apply to Ricky's gun? I certainly don't know how to disassemble a gun, but just holding it gives me a strange thrill.

It makes me feel powerful.

And I like it.

It aligns with my new life filled with empowerment and optimism. I have friends and the New Soundz. They are becoming my family. And Drake is becoming my boyfriend. My first boyfriend since my divorce. Joe isn't the only one who can move on. I'm moving on too—with someone better.

I'll talk to Drake about an outing. He has a car and could drive us there. Or I could buy a car or I could go back to the airport in San Jose and drive mine back to Vegas. It would be useful to have a car if I plan to stay in Las Vegas for a lot longer. Would I stay a lot longer? *What do you think, Rochelle?* What would be left for me without the New Soundz residency? *Drake.* I don't think I can count on that. Especially if I'll need a quick departure from Las Vegas in the event they find out about the gun. But if they don't, maybe I'll get a job on the next residency. Who knows who might come next? Maybe Kelly Clarkson? Or another great singer?

This could be the start of such a beautiful future.

But first, I have to get rid of the gun. I certainly don't need to end up in jail for theft. It would ruin everything I have planned.

I'm about to call Drake about the Lake Mead trip when my phone buzzes.

I look at the screen.

It isn't him.

It's Kayci. I haven't spoken to anyone from back home since I arrived in Las Vegas two weeks ago. Just a few texts and pictures from the Strip and a few selfies during a rehearsal.

For a moment, I hesitate, staring at the buzzing phone. Am I ready to chat with someone from my old life? I have to be. She's one of my closest friends.

I answer, "Hi, Kayci."

"Hi, Jess! How are you?"

"I'm doing well. How are you? How are the kids?"

"All is good around here. I thought I'd give you a call. Your pix are amazing. I'm so jealous. How's Las Vegas?"

"It's amazing!" I say, forcing excitement into my words. And I tell her everything—well, most of it. I talk about my new job and my new boyfriend, leaving out the part about the gun, Ricky, and my plans for justice.

"A boyfriend already?" she says, a note of surprise in her voice. "That's... incredible. I'm happy for you! How many times have you and Drake gone out?"

I pause to think. "I don't know. Officially, maybe five or six times. But we work together, so it's like twenty dates if you count all the hours we've spent together."

Silence on the other end.

Finally, Kayci says, "Oh, that's great. What's he like?"

"He's really nice and a bit older."

"Oh," she says. "How much older?"

"He's about to turn fifty." And as I say it, I realize she might be surprised by his age, and, honestly, I wouldn't date another man that old if it wasn't for the mission. Not after being with Joe, with all his "When you're my age" nonsense and his belief he was always right simply because he was older. I add, "I know I said I didn't want another Joe, but Drake doesn't look his age. I wouldn't have gone for him if he did!" The truth is Drake definitely looks his age. And I realize I can lie about this because it's likely Kayci will never meet him. It's kind of sad, but most likely true.

Kayci says, "Well, if you're happy, I'm happy."

"I am," I say, although it's not exactly true. I'd be a lot happier if Ricky hadn't realized his gun was missing.

"That's great."

And there is a lull because I can't tell her the truth. No one can know about the gun or the plan. "Kayci, it was so good to hear from you," I say. "But I have to go. We'll talk later, okay? I'll text you."

She says goodbye, and I end the call. A bit of sadness washes over me as I realize I may never go back to my old life in California. Most of it I don't want, but there were a few bits I did like.

Like Kayci and Sophie. With any new beginning, there are naturally going to be some endings you don't anticipate.

Trying to shake off the heavy feelings, I turn my thoughts to my next move. With the New Soundz blaring from my phone speakers, I sway to the music and suddenly a new thought slams into me, sharp and electric.

It's perfect.

It's brilliant.

It could solve all my problems.

My lips curl into a smile, the tension in my chest easing as excitement takes over. I hurry into the bedroom and open the drawer, pull off the towel, and stare down at the gun. "It's time the two of us get to know each other better."

CHAPTER THIRTY-SEVEN

Practically skipping down the Strip, I head out for an evening of errands. The neon lights shimmer all around, telling me the universe is on my side, guiding me toward my destiny. But then I see him—*Ricky*.

He is walking with a young blonde, her hair flowing in a cascade of loose curls and her face painted to perfection. She can't be more than twenty. The girl looks like she could be a showgirl in training with her skimpy top and micro-mini skirt. I'm not judging her. She does what she has to do to survive. If that means dating an icky dude like Ricky, more power to her. I only hope she is safe and knows what she is doing.

Does she think Ricky is creepy? He has to be at least sixty. The thought of him anywhere near her makes my stomach churn. He could be her grandfather. And yet, there he is, leaning too close, his gaze lingering far too long on each of her curves.

I feel a thrill of righteous indignation burn through me. This is exactly the kind of ammunition I need. I slip my phone from my bag and snap a photo of them, pretending to fidget with it as they continue down the Strip.

Look at this dirty old man with a poor young girl who's just trying to get by.

It will be perfect for the FB group I am putting together to expose Ricky for the sleaze he is.

I tip down my baseball cap and quicken my pace, blending into the flow of tourists as I follow them. They don't go far, turning into the MGM Grand. I hesitate at the entrance. Is he staying in the same hotel as the New Soundz residency? Or just getting something to eat? Either way, I need to know.

I step inside, keeping a safe distance. Ricky is too enamored with the young woman to notice me—or anyone else, for that matter. The way he ogles her and casually touches her shoulder makes me want to vomit. She flinches slightly when his hand slides down her back, his fingers brushing her spine like some predator marking his prey. Perhaps she is indeed *working*.

I follow them to a noodle shop tucked into the corner of the casino. Not the easiest place to blend in, but Ricky isn't paying attention to anyone except her. Once they are seated, I walk in and ask for a table for one.

Luck is on my side. The young woman faces me, while Ricky has his back to me. He will never even know I was there.

I sit down, pulling out my phone and pretending to scroll. My thumb hovers over the video button, and I hit record. Through the screen, I watch them—Ricky leaning across the table, speaking animatedly, and the girl nodding out of politeness. Her body language screams discomfort, but he is too self-absorbed to notice.

The server comes, and I order a bowl of noodles, acting as inconspicuous as possible. I turn my attention back to my phone, watching and recording, but the scene isn't giving me much to work with.

My noodles arrive, steaming and smelling of chili and garlic.

Yum. I set my phone down since I'm not getting much usable footage anyway and take a bite as I focus on my plan.

While I eat, I pull up Google Maps and start searching for the supplies I'll need for my new and *improved* plan. It's all mapped out. I'll hit multiple shops to avoid suspicion. A tiny liquor store that sells burner phones next to a fast-food place will be perfect. It will look like I'm popping in for snacks, not plotting something bigger.

The noodles are surprisingly delicious, the perfect distraction from the restless energy humming inside me. I glance over at Ricky and the girl again.

She has only ordered a small plate of spring rolls. She barely touches them, her fingers picking at the edge of her napkin while Ricky talks and laughs, oblivious to her discomfort.

My heart beats faster, my grip tightening on the chopsticks. She doesn't want to be there. I know it. But what can I do? Confront him here? No, that would ruin everything.

Finishing my noodles, I reach for my phone again, watching and waiting for the next move. The gears in my mind spin faster, each thought darker, sharper.

This isn't just about Ricky anymore.

It is about power. Control. Justice.

And I will get it. One way or another.

There isn't much else to see for now, but maybe I can find out where they are heading next. I don't know if Ricky is staying at the hotel or just having dinner. Either way, I want to learn more about his habits—what he does after work, where he spends his evenings.

With my noodles gone, I wait for the bill and watch as the young woman barely touches her food, only gingerly nibbling at the corner of a roll. Ricky, on the other hand, shovels food into his mouth without a care, oblivious to how utterly revolting he is.

I glance at her, and for a fleeting moment, our eyes meet. She looks at me, wide-eyed, almost pleading, I think, and I quickly turn away, pretending to be absorbed in my phone. I scroll through TikTok and Instagram, pretending to laugh at some meaningless video. But my heart is racing.

Does she know I'm watching?

Does she want me to be watching?

Is this her first *date*? She certainly doesn't seem like a seasoned pro, but then again, I don't know many of those—or any, really.

The chipper server arrives at my table, and I pay the bill. I quietly leave the restaurant and wander back into the casino. At the first set of slots, I sit and slip a bill into the machine. To my surprise, I win the first round. It isn't much, just enough to believe it's another sign that the universe is on my side. *Don't you think, Rochelle?*

I cash out and keep an eye on the noodle shop. Sure enough, Ricky and the young woman emerge, heading toward the elevators. My heart races with anticipation. I follow at a distance, walking slowly behind other casino patrons, trying to be invisible to Ricky.

When they reach the elevator bank, Ricky presses the button, his hand casually brushing her back again. She doesn't flinch this time, but her body is stiff.

There are other people waiting at the elevator—an elderly couple, a businessman, and me. I keep my head low, my cap tilted just enough to obscure my face. The elevator doors open, and we all shuffle inside.

I slip in behind the elderly couple, positioning myself just right. Ricky doesn't even glance back. He thinks he is safe and there is no need to worry about being followed. *Not so, Ricky.*

The elevator stops, and Ricky and the girl step off. A heartbeat later, I follow, stalling near the first room number directory to give me some distance. Neither Ricky nor his date notice me. I keep on pretending to check the room numbers on the wall as I walk.

The woman glances back at me. *Dang it.* I look away immediately, acting as if I'm lost. I slow down, pretending to study the room signs more closely before turning back toward the elevators for a quick escape.

But then, I hear Ricky call out, "Hey, you! Right there. Stop!" And the sound of their footsteps hurrying toward me.

This is bad. Very bad.

CHAPTER THIRTY-EIGHT

I freeze for a split second, then turn to face Ricky, forcing a casual smile. "Oh, hey!" I say, as if we're old friends bumping into each other by accident.

His eyes narrow, suspicious. "I know you. You're that girl from hospitality. Why are you following us?"

Girl? I'm thirty-five years old, almost thirty-six. I'm hardly *a girl*.

"Following you?" I shake my head. "I'm not following you. I didn't even notice you, actually."

The young woman folds her arms, glaring at me. "She's lying. She was at the noodle place too."

I shrug, playing it off. "So? I had noodles, played the machines afterward, and now I'm on my way to my friend's room. Nothing to do with you. I even won, like, sixty bucks. You can check my ticket."

Ricky's gaze hardens. "Something's off about you."

I remain silent.

"I'm gonna call security," Ricky says, pulling out his phone.

My stomach tightens. "That's not necessary!" I snap, a little too quickly. "This is ridiculous. I'm just here to see a friend."

Ricky tilts his head, his expression skeptical. "What friend?"

My brain scrambles for an answer. I can't give him a man's name. If Ricky tells Drake, it could ruin everything. He would think I'm seeing someone else. He might think I'm lying to him. And if that happens... No. That can't happen. That would destroy us.

I plaster on a fake smile. "Look, I think I'm on the wrong floor. She said it was floor 23, and this is 22," I say, backing toward the elevator.

"Yeah, right," the girl mutters under her breath, rolling her eyes.

Ricky's fingers hover over his phone screen. "I don't think so," he says.

But before he can make the call, the elevator doors open with a soft chime. Without thinking, I dart inside, jabbing the close button frantically. Ricky takes a step forward, but the doors slide shut just as he reaches them.

I lean against the wall, my chest heaving, as the elevator descends. My heart pounds so loudly it drowns out the soft rock music overhead. That was close—too close.

My hands tremble as I adjust my cap. What is wrong with me? I haven't planned this at all. I just saw an opportunity and acted on instinct.

It was reckless. Stupid. Amateur.

For a moment, self-doubt creeps in. But then, just as quickly, I shove it aside.

This is only a hiccup. A misstep. And I am far too close to stop now.

CHAPTER THIRTY-NINE

At work a few days later, I make a point of avoiding Ricky. I need to act as normal as possible—friendly but not overly so, just like I always have.

To sell it, I wear the baseball cap again, making it look like it's just a casual part of my wardrobe. In truth, I've started wearing it on purpose to run errands and avoid facial recognition cameras. Not that anyone needs to know that.

I'm in Ethan's dressing room, setting down a vase of fresh flowers, when I hear footsteps echoing down the hall. I panic at first, but soon realize the steps aren't coming toward me. They're storming off in the opposite direction, heavy and purposeful.

Somebody's in a mood.

I exhale, relieved it wasn't someone coming for me. Ignoring the thought, I focus on the long to-do list Gianni gave me—determined to finish every item. I love my job here—every part of it. The team feels like family. It's not just work; it's my home, my haven.

I'm just about to check off the last item on the list when Drake and Gianni walk up to me. Their expressions are serious, their postures stiff.

"Hi, Gianni. Hi, Drake," I say, forcing a sweet smile. "What's up?"

Gianni doesn't return my smile. He barely even looks at me. "We need to speak with you."

The panic returns. "What about?"

"Come with us," Gianni says, motioning toward his office.

Drake doesn't say anything. He just keeps his gaze averted, his face unreadable.

Oh no.

My mind races as I follow them down the hallway to Gianni's office. What could this be about? Did someone see Drake and me kissing the other day? Is it against company policy for coworkers to date?

The thought makes my stomach twist.

That's it. It has to be. They found out about us.

Gianni gestures for me to take a seat, and Drake sits beside me. The air in the office is tense, and neither of them look very happy.

I force myself to sit still, though my hands itch to fidget. My heart hammers in my chest as I glance between them.

Apprehensively, I watch as Gianni takes a seat behind his desk. He leans back, folding his hands as his gaze settles on me.

"Well," he says. "This is not the way I like to start my day."

"What's going on? Is everything okay?"

I glance at Drake, searching for reassurance, but he won't meet my eyes. I offer him a small, hopeful smile, but he doesn't return it.

Gianni sighs. "I'm just going to come out and say it."

"Say what?"

"We have to let you go, Jess."

The words hit me like a punch to the stomach. I blink, uncomprehending. "I don't understand. Why?"

Gianni's face remains impassive. "Your employment is at-will. We don't have to give you a reason, but you'll get your last paycheck in the next day or two. We have your address on file—you're still staying at the Hyatt, right?"

"Yes, but—" My voice cracks. "I don't understand. Do you think I'm not doing a good job?"

"It's not that."

I shake my head, refusing to accept it. "Is this because of Drake and me?"

Gianni's brow furrows. "What about you and Drake?"

Drake rests his hand on my arm, and he says, "Jess and I have gone out a few times."

Gianni's jaw tightens, his expression shifting to one of surprise. "No. It's not that."

"If it's not because I'm doing a bad job or dating Drake, then what? I don't understand!" *The gun. The encounter with Ricky at the hotel. Could it be that? Or is it Mario trying to get rid of me? He wouldn't, would he? Not Mario.*

Gianni holds up a hand. "Please, Jess. Make this easier for all of us and just pack up your things. I'm guessing you don't have much. We'll need you to leave immediately."

My breath catches, panic rising in my throat. "You're throwing me out?" My voice cracks, growing louder. "How can you do this? I've been an excellent employee!"

"Jess," Gianni says firmly. "I'm asking you to leave. If you can't do that, I'll have to call security."

"Security? I'm one of you!"

Drake places a hand on my shoulder, but I yank it away. "This is outrageous!"

Gianni continues, "This is your last chance to go before I call security."

I feel the walls closing in, my chest tight as if the air has been sucked out of the room.

Drake says, "Come on, Jess. Let's go."

He ushers me out of the office, his hand lightly gripping my elbow. My steps are heavy as I force myself to leave.

"I just need to grab my bag."

Drake nods. "Come on. Get your bag, and I'll walk you out."

I stop abruptly, turning to him. "Do you know why this is happening?"

He avoids my eyes, shaking his head. "Let's just go."

What? He knows and won't tell me?

We walk in silence to the back exit, fury building inside me. Drake holds the door open, with only the empty street waiting for me.

He hesitates, his voice low. "I'll talk to you later."

Before I can say anything, the door shuts behind me with a heavy thud.

I stand there, alone on the side street. My body rocks lightly as the weight of it all crashes down on me. Anger. Disappointment. Disbelief. Why have they done this to me? Who did this to me? *It's all falling apart, Rochelle.* One thing I *do* know is that I *will* find out who did this to me, and they will *pay*.

CHAPTER FORTY

The anger quickly turns into defeat, and I stumble back to my hotel room as tears stream down my face. Nobody stops me or asks if I'm okay. Maybe they're looking at me, pointing. Or they're too busy thinking about the next casino to hit, the next overly sweet alcoholic slushy to gulp down. The rest of the world feels so distant, like I no longer belong in it.

When I reach my room, I drop my bag with a heavy thud just inside the door and trudge toward the bedroom. My legs feel like lead, every step harder than the last. I collapse onto the bed, face-first into the pillows, muffling the choked sobs I can't hold back.

Everything is falling apart. My plans, my life, everything. I've been exiled. Cast out like garbage. But why? The only thing willing me to continue on is the anger I feel toward whomever got me fired.

Mario. It has to be him. He wanted me gone because he doesn't want me telling his secrets. But would he really do that to me? Mario? The thought twists my stomach into knots so tight I think I might vomit. A black hole of despair fills me, pulling everything down into its suffocating void. I feel like I'm disappearing, being erased.

The last time I felt so lost and hopeless was when Joe dumped me. I thought my world had ended, but that was different. That pain was sharp, bitter, but survivable. This is something else entirely—shattering and all-consuming, a pain so deep I can't see a way out.

My body shakes with silent heaves until, finally, I still. I wipe my face with trembling hands and sit up.

My reflection in the darkened window startles me. My eyes are swollen, my hair tangled like a wild animal. I look deranged. *Am I, Rochelle?*

Then it hits me. *Hard.*

The last time I felt like this was when I was sixteen years old. A letter from Rochelle had arrived that day. Another letter filled with...

I shiver, clutching the edge of the bed as the old memories seep back into me like poison.

When I saw the envelope, I was happy but apprehensive at the same time. My hands shook as I opened it, a mix of hope and dread coiling in my stomach. Rochelle's words were like shards of glass slicing through me. Every sentence brought more darkness, filling every cell in my body with an unbearable heaviness.

It was a goodbye.

She never wrote the word outright, but I could feel it in every line. She was done. She couldn't hold on anymore. The grief and the shame of what had happened to her, had consumed her—eating away at her, bite by bite, until there was nothing left.

Twice I tried to call her, desperate to hear her voice, to say something—anything—that might bring her back to me. But Rochelle never answered.

When my mother came home from work, I begged her to

drive me to see Rochelle. I told her it was an emergency, that it couldn't wait. But she waved me off. "Stop being so dramatic, Jessica," she snapped. "Grow up and focus on what's important—helping me put food on the table and taking care of your sister."

She didn't understand. She didn't care. She couldn't see how much I was suffering. But Rochelle was suffering even more. It was like when we were separated, someone had cut our shared lifeline. We were both fading, slowly and painfully.

I didn't know if I could go on without Rochelle in my life. She was all I had—the only person who truly understood me. And yet, after that letter, she never sent another. And then there was the phone call...

Looking back, I know part of me died that day, and I wanted to give up on the fight. To stop trying to be different than my mother. It seemed too hard to do it all alone. I thought I wasn't strong enough. Without Rochelle, my joy and hope drained away. Rochelle was gone, and I was left with nothing.

Eventually, I broke out of the darkness and forged ahead with school and college. I met Kayci and Sophie and eventually Joe. *Joe. Ick.* He gave me just enough to make me feel good about myself, but not enough to let me believe I could be without him. It's strange how everything can seem so perfect and rosy, only for a storm to set in and wash away that pretty picture.

Maybe the fight in me is really gone this time. They've all beaten it out of me—Rochelle, Joe, my mother, Mario, and Ricky. Every single one of them.

I can still expose Ricky, but what will it matter? Does anyone care? Would anyone care if I were gone?

The sadness is suffocating and consuming me whole. My chest feels heavy, my breaths shallow. I can barely breathe. The defeat is unbearable, and I can't handle it anymore.

I climb off the bed, my legs shaky, and make my way to the kitchen. I don't know why—just that I have to go, to do something, to stop feeling everything all at once.

I pull a bottle of wine from the fridge. It's almost full. I don't bother with a glass, just twist the stopper off and drink.

And drink.

And drink.

The burn in my throat dulls the ache in my chest, numbing the edges of my mind. It doesn't hurt anymore.

For a moment, it's quiet.

And that quiet feels like salvation, and I think, *I'll leave revenge for another day—if there's another day.*

CHAPTER FORTY-ONE

An annoying buzzing sound pulls me out of unconsciousness. My head throbs, and my mouth feels like sandpaper. The noise persists, sharp and grating, like a drill boring into my skull. I glance over at the coffee table. My phone. Someone is calling me.

I groan and reach for it, squinting at the screen. The name "Drake" glows back at me. Surprising, really. When I open the notifications, I see he's called several times. What does *he* want?

The phone buzzes again in my hand, but I ignore it, tossing it back onto the table. My eyes drift to the empty bottle of wine. I reach for it, tilting it, but not even a drop is left.

Frustration bubbles inside me. With a sudden, reckless motion, I hurl the bottle across the room. It shatters against the wall, glass shards scattering like tiny, sharp stars. I stare at the mess. I should care. I should clean it up. But I don't.

It's hard to care about anything anymore. I am alone in this world, and the only reason I've survived this long is because I was young and scrappy, full of pluck. Or so they said. But life has beaten it all out of me.

My last attempt at something stable, something real, was a life with Joe. *Fail.* He was no big loss, I can see that now, but a year ago, I thought he was my everything. Until he left too. The life I built with him is gone, just another illusion crumbling to dust. Another person to leave me.

I thought maybe, just maybe, there was hope again. But that hope has been stolen from me, just like everything else. Now, there is nothing left. Nothing ahead of me but a steep downhill spiral. And I am already sliding.

The phone buzzes again. It's Drake. I sigh heavily and pick it up, swiping to answer this time.

"Hello."

"Jess, are you okay?"

"I'm fine."

"I've been calling all day. I was worried."

I pull the phone away from my ear, staring at the time on the screen. It's noon. "I was busy."

There's a pause on the other end. Then he says, "Oh. I was thinking I could stop by if you wanted to talk."

Talk? Is that what he thinks I need? To talk. So he can pretend to care about me? He wouldn't have let them fire me if he cared. He wouldn't have left me sobbing alone in that alley if he cared. He was just like all the rest. Why did I ever think he could be different?

"Why?" I ask, my voice filled with anger. "Why did they fire me, Drake? Tell me that."

"I think it's best if we talk in person. Okay?"

"Fine," I snap, though I don't mean it. I don't care what he has to say or what anyone has to say.

I end the call and toss the phone aside, sinking back into the couch. The old-new me—strong and powerful Jess—is gone, and I hate who I've become. Weak, bitter, and utterly hollow. Again.

There is nothing left to fight for.

I stare at the shards of broken wine bottle scattered across the carpet. The jagged pieces glitter as the sunlight hits them. My eyes drift to the faint marks on the wall where the bottle had broken.

With a groan, I force myself upright and shuffle into the kitchen for paper towels. My body feels heavy and sluggish, as though I am wading through molasses. Carefully, I begin scooping up the larger shards, tossing them into the trash with a dull clink. The smaller bits can wait. The wall can wait. Everything can wait.

The buzz of my phone interrupts the silence again. I glance at the screen. It's Drake again. "Yes?"

"I'm downstairs. I'll be right up."

"Okay."

I hang up and wonder—what does he want with me, anyway? Staring at the mess, I realize maybe having him over isn't a great idea. I grab more paper towels and start cleaning up the smaller pieces, then try to get the red wine stains off the walls. Mid-wipe, the knock at the door startles me. I hesitate, staring at it.

I throw away the towel and go to open the door. I don't bother checking the peephole. It's Drake—or maybe it isn't. Maybe someone has finally come to attack me and finish me off. That fear is always there, lurking in the back of my mind. Would it be a blessing?

But when I open the door, there's Drake. There's a faint sparkle in his eyes, though it dims as he looks me over.

I open the door wider, stepping back. "Come in."

He steps inside, glancing around the room. His eyes linger on the sofa, and he makes his way there, sitting down cautiously, like he doesn't want to make himself too comfortable.

"Are you okay?"

"I had some wine," I say flatly, sitting down beside him. I

wonder briefly if my words are slurred. I could use another bottle.

Drake hesitates, studying my face. "I'm sorry about everything. About you being let go. I know you really liked the job."

"I didn't need the money," I say, my voice sharper than I intend. "But yeah, I liked it. So, why? Why did they fire me?"

He rubs the back of his neck, looking away for a moment. "I asked around. It was Ricky Star, the tour manager. You know who he is, right?"

"I do," I say, suddenly feeling the haze of the wine lift. My body tenses, an icy clarity washing over me. *Ricky.*

Drake sighs. "He said... well, he said he'd gotten complaints from Mario. That Mario thought you were, uh, weird."

Mario. "Weird?"

"Yeah. Ricky said Mario told him you gave off some kind of strange vibe. That you didn't fit with the crew."

"That doesn't even make sense," I snap. "Mario wouldn't say that. He wouldn't."

"Are you sure? I mean, did something happen between you and Mario? Or maybe between you and Ricky? A confrontation or something?"

I don't answer the question. My mind is racing, fitting the pieces together. "So, it was Ricky who insisted you fire me?"

"Yes. He's the boss. There was nothing any of us could do about it."

Ricky thinks he can silence me. He thinks he can just toss me aside, sweep me into the trash like I'm nothing. He thinks he can get away with all of it—his secrets, his sins, his lies.

He won't.

Not this time.

The deep sadness and sorrow that consumed me earlier begin to morph into something else. Rage. Pure, unfiltered rage. Ricky has gotten away with far too much for far too long.

"Are you sure you're okay?"

I turn to look at him. "I'm fine. Perfectly fine."

His brow furrows. "You don't seem fine. I'm really sorry about all of this, Jess."

"Don't be sorry," I say quickly, cutting him off. "I'll be fine."

But even as I say the words, I'm not sure what my plan is. Fine isn't an option anymore. Fine isn't enough. I don't just want to be okay—I want justice. Revenge. Ricky thinks he can get rid of me, thinks he can turn everyone against me—my New Soundz family, the crew, and even Drake.

He's wrong.

I will expose everything he's ever done, every lie and every crime. I will drag his dark deeds into the light for everyone to see. And I will do it for Rochelle. For the other women he's hurt. For myself.

Drake reaches out, placing a tentative hand on mine. I flinch instinctively, pulling away.

"I think you should go."

"What do you mean?"

"I'm just upset about all of this," I say, standing up and moving toward the door. "I just want to be alone."

"Are you sure?"

"Yes. I'm sure."

It isn't entirely a lie. I don't want Drake to see me fall apart. But more than that, I can't stand the thought of having him here, one of Ricky's puppets, just another person following orders. I need someone who can stand up for what's right, not someone who folds under Ricky's control. I guess my man-picker is off. I can't trust my instincts when it comes to the opposite sex. That is clear to me now.

As Drake hesitates by the door, I wish he could have been the man I thought he was. But if I'm being honest, I knew we'd never work out in the end.

Without another word, he leaves, and I know exactly what I have to do. I can't stay in this pit. I have to climb out. I have to fight—for what is right, for what is mine.

Ricky Star *will pay* for what he's done.

If it's the last thing I do.

CHAPTER FORTY-TWO

MARIO

Guilt is beginning to take over. I should never have said anything negative about Jess to Ricky. Not that what I said was anything too terrible, just that she gives me a strange vibe. That single comment set something terrible in motion, and now, there is no undoing it.

When Ricky pulled me into his office, I could tell he was upset about something. I had assumed it was something having to do with me, but I was wrong. Inside the confines of his office, he told me he saw Jess in the hallway of his hotel room and that her explanation was that she was on the wrong floor, but he didn't believe her. Ricky asked me if she ever gave me a weird vibe. Instead of shutting him down, I shrugged and said, "Maybe a little." It was a throwaway comment meant to shut down the conversation and to get away from Ricky. Truth was I didn't like him and never had.

But after the conversation, I was both surprised and a little worried. Was Jess trying to confront him? I wanted to ask her, but when I came into work the next day, she was gone. Fired. No explanation, just whispers backstage. The realization dawns on me that it was likely Ricky who was responsible. Jess was a victim of Ricky all those years ago, and now she's lost her job too. Her life turned upside down because of him—and because of me.

The guilt twists inside me as I sit in the quiet of my dressing room, the faint hum of activity in the hall outside. Suddenly, the door flies open, slamming against the wall with a bang that jolts me from my seat.

Ethan and Davey barge in, their faces flushed, their eyes wide.

"What's up, guys?"

"Did you see?" Ethan blurts out.

"See what?" I ask. The way they look at me, I know something bad is coming.

Davey's eyes are wide, his face pale. "Google Ricky Star."

My stomach clenches. My fingers tremble as I pull out my phone and open the search app. I type in his name, my pulse racing with every keystroke. The search results load, and there they are—article after article, headline after headline: "Ricky Star Accused of Sexual Assault."

"Decades of Abuse Allegations Against Ricky Star." "Ricky Star, a Pedophile, Lured Young Girls Under the Guise of Meeting the New Soundz."

I keep scrolling, unable to stop. Then I see a link to a Facebook group. I click on it.

The page loads, and the group's name makes my heart drop: *Justice for Victims of Ricky Star*. There are already 5,000 members.

The pinned comment at the top is from a woman named Delilah. Her post is simple but brutal. "I always knew Ricky Star was a creep back then. I'm surprised he still has a job with the New Soundz."

Other comments follow in a flood of outrage, speculation, and shared trauma. Someone claims it was all covered up, suggesting other band members or crew had to have known. One woman recounts her own experience from 1999, writing that she had been assaulted but had been too afraid to come forward at the time.

It is overwhelming—names, dates, accusations piling up. My chest tightens, and all I can think about is Jess, what happened to her friend, and the part I played in keeping it all under wraps.

Guilt is now all I can feel.

"Can you believe it?" Davey's voice pulls me out of the fog.

I glance over at him and Ethan. They stand there, both of them in full shock. We've been best friends for more than two decades, touring together, practically living with one another—and with Ricky Star.

Ethan breaks the silence. "Do you think it's true?"

I open my mouth, but no words come. Because deep down, I already know the answer. Have they really never seen him with one of those young women backstage? Or worse—with young girls who are *far* too young?

"It could be."

How much can I say? How much should I say? My mind races, balancing the need for truth against the fear of what Ricky might do to me—or worse, to my family. My partner, our son—they are innocent in all of this. I can't risk dragging them into it.

"Why?" Davey asks. "Did you ever see him with someone?"

I hesitate, the words sticking in my throat. "I've... I've seen him with young women," I admit finally, carefully choosing my words. "I don't know all the details, but I... I suspected he was *dating* a lot." I lift my hands, making air quotes around the word "dating."

Davey and Ethan exchange a look.

"Is he here?" I ask.

Davey says, "No, he didn't come in today."

"When did all this break?"

Ethan shifts uneasily. "Well, I just saw it this morning, but from what I found, the Facebook group started a couple of days ago. That's when the media picked up on it. And with the group growing, more and more women started coming forward. Now the FBI's investigating—human trafficking, sexual assault... Straight-up #MeToo."

The Facebook group started three days ago—Jess was fired four days ago. It has to be her handiwork.

At least Ricky is finally getting what he deserves. There is some solace in knowing that he won't be able to hurt anyone else. But the guilt still clings to me. Because I didn't stop him when I could have.

"This is shocking," I say, though it isn't the accusations themselves that stun me—it is that someone has finally come forward, pieced it all together, and exposed him. Someone with courage. *Jess*. "What are we supposed to do? Is the New Soundz going to put out a statement?" I ask.

"Yeah," Davey says. "Drake's already talking to our manager. They're putting a statement together for the press."

"What does the statement say?"

Ethan says, "That we had no knowledge of any of this and that we're distancing ourselves from him as much as possible. We don't want this in our lives—it could ruin us."

I swallow hard, the words twisting like a knife in my gut. It has already ruined lives—so many lives.

"And no one's talked to Ricky?" I ask, pulling out my phone. I glance at the screen—no new messages from him or anyone else.

Ethan says, "No. But man, it's crazy. This is Ricky. We worked with him for years. If the FBI's involved, they must have found something pretty bad."

"Maybe it's true," I say. "Maybe he did all those things. I don't think we should assume the women are making it up."

Ethan frowns. "But why now? Why come forward so many years later?"

I think back to my conversation with Jess. "Maybe they were scared."

"Scared?" Ethan scoffs. "He wasn't that intimidating. He's just a guy, right?"

But he had intimidated me. Blackmailed me. Threatened me. As a gay man in an industry built on the fantasy of us—the band members—falling in love with female fans, getting married, and living the perfect storybook life, Ricky had weaponized my secret. He had made sure I kept my mouth shut for years, dangling the truth over my head like a noose.

"Well, if the allegations are true and it's young girls..." Davey trails off, his face filled with doubt. "I mean, without proof, don't we have to keep an open mind?"

I shake my head. "Our fans gave us this life. Without them, we're nothing. We have to stand with them."

Davey hesitates, glancing at me. "Maybe you're right. Either way, we're still putting out the press release. Whether he's guilty or not, he must have pissed someone off for this to happen."

I nod absently, though my mind is elsewhere. "I've got to grab something to eat before rehearsal. Talk to you guys later."

They exchange a glance, clearly sensing something is off, but I don't give them a chance to press me. I have something to take care of—before it is too late.

CHAPTER FORTY-THREE

BACK FROM THE FIRING RANGE, I put the gun back inside the drawer next to the Bible. It was my third time, and I was feeling more confident that I could use it if I needed to. Most of my life I've been afraid of guns but now I know it's only because I'd never been taught how to handle one. It's safe if you treat it with respect. And now that I know how to shoot it, I feel changed. Truly powerful and in control. *Unstoppable.*

Amped from my outing, I feel ready to do what I've intended to do all along. With New Soundz turned up on the speaker, I curl up on the couch and open up the Facebook app on my phone and go immediately to the *Justice for Ricky Star's Victims* group. Since I created it, the posts have flooded in, one after another—stories, accusations, heartbreaks. There are so many victims and so many lives shattered by him. The weight of it is *crushing*.

And now it's time to tell Rochelle's story. But I can't use my own name or hers. I create a new profile, an anonymous voice to explain what Ricky has done to her, what he's taken from her. Rochelle is a victim, and in many ways, so am I. The guilt gnaws at me, as sharp now as it was then.

The thing about violent crime is that the victim isn't the only one who gets hurt. There's a ripple effect of heartbreak, guilt, and regret. Those of us who aren't attacked still carry the weight of wondering: What could I have done differently to prevent it from happening?

I think back to that night. I just sat there, waiting for Rochelle to return, thinking everything would be fine. It didn't make sense then, and it doesn't make sense now. What if I'd been less timid? What if I'd gone looking for her? What if I'd protected her? *What ifs* twenty years later weren't helpful.

But now, I can do something. I can tell her story, even if she isn't here to tell it herself. I owe her that much.

I don't use her real name. Rochelle has family, and if they see it—if they don't know what happened—I'm not going to be the one to force that truth onto them. It isn't my place.

I type out the post, my fingers trembling as I write. The details spill out in halting, careful phrases. What was done to her. How it was swept under the rug. How the system and those around her failed her.

When I finish, I click Post.

Within minutes, the notifications start. Likes. Comments. Messages of support. People share their outrage, their empathy. It makes me wonder. If social media had been what it is today could we have stopped Ricky earlier? Back then, what did we have? Letters? Telephone calls? Chat rooms? MySpace? The tools to reach others across the world weren't like they are now. This was before social media took over our lives and the smartphone became a new appendage. Now everyone has a camera ready—each recording events and uploading them to the web or their favorite app in moments. What if we'd had it back then?

The flood of messages from other survivors, each telling their stories, each echoing the pain Ricky has caused, only deepens my regret. I should have done this sooner.

It's not like I forgot what had happened. Rather, I chose to bury it because the pain of remembering was too much to bear. But now it's out there. Everyone will know. *Rochelle, you have a voice.*

The world finally knows who Ricky Star really is.

Twenty-plus years of abuse. Decades of stealing lives, innocence, and hope. His victims are coming forward, and they're going to make him pay.

And I'm going to make sure he gets what he deserves.

I Google Ricky Star's name again, desperate for updates on the case. It's everywhere, dominating the headlines, "Ricky Star Exposed as a Predator."

Every major outlet is covering it, analyzing the fallout. A new article catches my eye—a press release from the New Soundz. My stomach twists as I read their carefully worded statement, "We had no knowledge of any wrongdoing by Ricky Star. The band is deeply shocked and saddened by these allegations."

The words blur on the screen as my rage bubbles up, hot and unrelenting.

They knew. Of course they knew.

Mario knew.

As much as I love him—trust him—Mario betrayed me. He betrayed Rochelle, and he betrayed all the women Ricky hurt. He might've been blackmailed, and he might've been threatened, but that doesn't make it right. It doesn't erase the years of silence.

How is Mario feeling now? Is he panicking, worried I'll expose his part in all of this? Does he suspect it's me who set up the Facebook group, who helped ignite the firestorm of accountability that is now consuming Ricky?

They tried to silence me. They couldn't. Not now. *Not in this era.*

I glance around my small, isolated room, knowing that I have been exiled from the New Soundz community. Fired. Disconnected. But it doesn't matter anymore because I have a new community. One I created myself, one that isn't just about me.

The Facebook group has thousands of members already—thousands of voices rising up, sharing stories, demanding justice. This is where I belong. Maybe it always has been.

It's not just Rochelle, or even Ricky, anymore. This is bigger. This is about all the victims. The forgotten ones. The silenced ones. And the predators who think they can get away with it. *Ricky is just the first.*

I set my phone down, the possibilities racing through my mind. Maybe this is my calling. Finding men like Ricky—men who prey on the vulnerable. There are so many predators out there. I know it because I've seen them. Just in my own small world, I've encountered more than a few. If there are this many in my orbit, how many more are lurking out there, unchecked?

The idea takes root, growing fast and strong. I can do it. I can expose them, one by one. The predators, the enablers, all of them. Justice won't stop with Ricky Star.

I clench my fists, a fiery determination within me. I thought I'd lost everything—my career, my purpose, my identity—when I was fired from the New Soundz. But maybe losing that life and that connection is the best thing that could've happened.

Drake? Mario? They are weak, bowing down to Ricky, protecting their own skins. They aren't to be trusted. But this new group. These survivors. These warriors for justice. They are my family now.

My old life in California—it all led me here. To this moment. This purpose.

This is my true calling. *I'm right, aren't I, Rochelle?*

I have to remember there's always hope. *Always.* Even in

the darkest of dark moments. It's something I tried so hard to convince Rochelle of, but she didn't believe me. Back then, I guess it felt like empty words. Now, I know it's real. Hope doesn't die. It just occasionally needs a spark to bring it back to life.

My phone vibrates on the couch beside me, the screen lighting up with an unfamiliar number. I stare at it, letting the call go to voicemail. I'm not interested in hearing from anyone I don't know. Who could it be?

I've been ignoring emails and calls from my former employer, my therapist's office, and from Drake. He's called multiple times, but I haven't answered. I don't need him anymore. He's not the man I hoped he was.

I have my new community—a group of survivors, advocates, and truth-seekers. I am safe here, alone in my hotel, away from the predators. I don't need love from a man anymore—it isn't enough, anyway. I want something more. Something bigger.

That's where I went wrong before, thinking too small. I wanted justice for Rochelle. I wanted to free the New Soundz from Ricky Star's poisonous grip. But justice shouldn't stop there. Everyone deserves to live without fear. Everyone deserves to be loved and respected—not treated like property, not told how to look, act, or behave by some creep who wants to control them.

It's time to think bigger. *Much bigger*.

The alert for a new voicemail breaks through my thoughts. Someone has left a message. Out of sheer curiosity, I pick up my phone and play the message. As the words spill through the speaker, my heart starts to pound. The voice is clear, confident, and it is saying exactly what I need to hear.

By the time the voicemail ends, a grin spreads across my face. I don't even hesitate. I call them back immediately, my fingers vibrating as I hit the dial button.

This isn't a coincidence.
This is destiny.
And this is just the beginning.

CHAPTER FORTY-FOUR

MARIO

THANKFULLY, nobody spots me on the street. The dark hat and oversized sunglasses help, along with keeping my head down. Not that I get recognized all that much anymore. It's not like the old days, when we couldn't step out of our homes without paparazzi or fans swarming us with signs reading "I heart Mario" and "New Soundz Forever." Back then, even a quick trip to the grocery store was an ordeal. Now, I can pretty much go anywhere without being recognized.

Still, I took extra precautions tonight. I'm not just out for a stroll. I'm heading to a hotel, and I don't want anyone asking why. If a photographer snaps my picture, the questions will start. "Why was Mario of the New Soundz sneaking into a hotel?"

The elevator ride up to Jess's room feels ominous. My mind is spinning, rehearsing what I'll say, how I'll plead with her. I'm almost certain she's the one behind the Facebook group exposing Ricky and everything he's done. And as much as I want to see Ricky held accountable, I can't let her expose me too.

I swallow hard as the elevator dings and the doors slide

open. The hallway is chilly and quiet. My steps are slow as I make my way to her room. My nerves are rattling as I stop in front of the door, raise a shaky hand, and knock.

The door opens almost immediately. Jess stands there in a pair of skinny jeans and a New Soundz sweatshirt.

The sweatshirt. I'll have to use that to my advantage. She was a huge fan once and I suspect she still is. Surely she doesn't want to destroy us—or me. At least, I hope not.

"Hi, Jess."

"Come in," she says, her voice chipper.

That's a good sign, isn't it?

I step into the room, which is larger than I was expecting. A kitchenette and living area separated from the bedroom made it feel less intimate, less awkward. At least we won't be perched on a bed, staring at each other, like I feared.

Jess gestures toward the couch. "Have a seat. Can I get you something? Coffee? Tea? Wine? I don't think I have any beer, though. Do you like beer?"

"Uh, maybe just water? Do you have water?" I ask, my throat suddenly dry.

"Of course." She smiles and heads toward the kitchenette.

She seems happy to see me, which gives me a shred of hope. Maybe she knows I'm on her side. If not, I'll do whatever it takes to get through to her. Anything she wants—anything she needs—I'll do it.

Jess returns to the sofa and sits down across from me, handing me the glass of water. She holds her own glass and turns slightly to face me, her expression unreadable.

"I was surprised to hear from you," she says. "But I'm really glad you reached out. How are you?"

"I'm doing well," I say, taking a sip of water to steady myself. "Things are a bit crazy around the office, as you can imagine."

She tilts her head, giving me a strange look. "I'd imagine it's more than a bit crazy—what with your tour manager being investigated by the FBI and all."

I nod, swallowing hard. "Since the news about Ricky broke... it's been hard. He's been accused of assaulting women—young girls, too—for decades. There's a Facebook group dedicated to his victims. It's been growing quickly." I keep my eyes on her face, searching for any sign of recognition, any flicker of guilt. The timing of it all is too perfect. I am certain she is behind it.

"Yes, I saw the press release," she says coolly.

There is something off in her demeanor. Is she testing me? "Well," I begin, "before we get into all that, there's something I need to talk to you about."

"Oh?" She raises her eyebrows.

"I heard you were fired," I say. "And... I also heard that Ricky was the one who requested it."

Jess's grip on her glass tightens, her knuckles whitening. Her face flushes an alarming shade of pink, darkening quickly to maroon. I need to speed this up. "He told me he convinced Drake that it was what we both wanted," I add quickly, trying to explain myself before her anger boils over. "But I want you to know, it was never my intention. I'm so sorry you were fired. Truly. I want to apologize for that."

Jess sets her glass down, her hands trembling slightly. "I was very upset by that. And yes, I did hear from Drake that it was you and Ricky who wanted me gone. As you can imagine, since I loved that job—and I love the New Soundz—that was *heartbreaking* for me."

There is a deep sadness in her eyes, one that seems to run deeper than whatever has happened in the short time I have known her.

"I'm very, very sorry," I say, leaning forward. "I've talked to the guys, and they're sorry too. I also talked to Drake, and if you want to come back, you can. He's okay with it—especially now that Ricky is gone." I had begged Drake to give me Jess's number so I could try to fix this because I need her back on my side. I need to rebuild the trust, so she won't expose my role in Ricky's crimes.

Jess blinks, clearly caught off guard. "Really? Drake said that?"

"Yes. He's worried about you. He hopes bringing you back will cheer you up. He said you haven't been returning his calls."

She glances away. "Yeah, I just... haven't really felt like talking to anyone."

"I understand. If there's anything I can do to help, please let me know."

She returns her focus to me. "Well, you've already done a lot. I really appreciate you getting my old job back, but I'll have to think about it."

"Of course. Take all the time you need." But I can't relax—not yet. I had expected Jess to be over the moon about the offer to come back. Her lukewarm response has caught me off guard. Is there something I don't know? "Do what's best for you, Jess. But just know—you're the best at what you do. Anything we ever needed, you were always right there. That didn't go unnoticed. We all really liked working with you."

She nods slowly. "Like I said, I'll think about it."

Her tone is polite but distant, and the tension in the air is growing heavy.

"Anything else?" she asks.

I hesitate. "Yeah, there's... another matter I want to talk to you about."

Her expression doesn't change, but I can feel her walls go up. "What is it?"

"That Facebook group for Ricky's victims..."

"What about it?"

"Well... I thought maybe you knew something about it."

Jess tilts her head slightly, her eyes narrowing as she studies me. She is sizing me up, deciding whether to trust me. "I've seen it," she says. "I noticed people are sharing their stories, and I think it's great. Victims are getting a voice, and they deserve that." She pauses and then says, "You're afraid. You're afraid I'm going to tell everyone that you knew about it."

Her words hit me hard. "Yes."

She stares out the window, looking out at the lights of the Strip, as if lost in thought. The silence is unnerving. I shift uncomfortably, feeling like a child waiting to be scolded.

Finally, she turns her attention back to me. "So, that's why you came by? Why you called? Why you got my job back? Are you bribing me to keep quiet? Just like you kept quiet all those years for Ricky? Like you're still keeping quiet now?"

I flinch.

She doesn't stop. "I saw the press release. It said you had no knowledge of what Ricky was doing. But you knew, didn't you?"

It's time to come clean. "The other guys really didn't know," I say. "They were shocked when the news broke. But me... I didn't dismiss the allegations. Because I knew. The other guys didn't."

Jess goes quiet again and she stares out the window once more. I can't tell what she's thinking, but I know she is contemplating something.

After what feels like hours, she turns back to me. "I understand your concerns. From the very beginning, I wanted to protect you—all of you. I knew Ricky could tarnish your good name, and I wanted to help get justice for Rochelle. I still want that." She pauses, her eyes meeting mine. "I will always be your number-one fan." She hesitates again and says, "But this is bigger than me. Bigger than you. It'd be so easy for me to type one comment into that Facebook group, to say I have inside knowledge that Mario knew about Ricky Star's crimes and that he was being blackmailed to keep quiet. That would be a huge story, wouldn't it?"

Her tone isn't totally threatening, but it's clear she knows she's holding all the power. She wants something—but what?

Jess leans back, crossing her arms as her eyes bore into mine. "I see you're willing to do something for me," she says. "Getting my job back, restoring my good name, bringing me back into the fold. I used to have a successful, lucrative career, but I never loved a job more than when I was working with all of you. Even though it was chaotic—crazy, really—in some ways, there was a beauty in the simplicity of it. Just helping incredible people connect with other people. It was special."

I nod slightly, unsure where she is going with this but sensing there is more.

"But the world is bigger than me, and I see that now. And I really, really want to expose Ricky for what he's done. He doesn't deserve to get away with it. Not anymore. To really do that, though, I need your help. And if you help me, I *can* keep your secret. If not..."

My stomach twists into a knot. "What exactly do you want me to do?"

A small smile forms on her lips, and something in her expression sends a chill down my spine.

CHAPTER FORTY-FIVE

More than ever, I understand my purpose on this earth. With the help of Mario and the New Soundz, this is just the beginning—the genesis of something incredible. An unstoppable movement. And Mario is willing to help. *Good for him.* Otherwise I'd have no choice but to expose him. It certainly isn't what I want to do. I do love him, despite his selfish nature. He was clearly only looking out for himself, but he is *just a man* after all. Not the god I thought he and the rest of the New Soundz were. And like every other man I've ever known, he's disappointed me. Despite that, I have to believe he'll go through with his promise and that everything will fall into place exactly as I have planned.

I've been knocked down before, *hard*, but I've always gotten back up. This time is no different. And I realize now that my mission has consumed me, so much I hadn't even stopped to grasp the absurdity of having Mario from the New Soundz sitting in my hotel room, talking to me. Sharing stories, secrets, and offering me my job back. *It was straight crazy, right, Rochelle?*

As much as I loved that job—and I truly had loved it—I

couldn't go back. I couldn't go *backward*. My path is leading me forward, and I have too much to do to prepare for what is coming next.

This isn't just about me. This is about justice. This is for all the victims of Ricky Star. They deserve to be believed, to have their stories validated and their pain recognized. And with Mario's help, I am going to make that happen.

Together, Mario and I will make sure the truth comes out.

And if he doesn't follow through with his end of the bargain —that's always a possibility considering what he's done in the past—Mario *will* suffer. *Dearly.* I truly hope that's not how our story ends.

My phone buzzes. Another text message. I sigh and open the text from Drake.

> Hey Jess, how are you? I've been really worried about you.

I stare at the screen for a moment before replying.

> You know, at first, I wasn't doing very well. But now I'm great. I've turned over a new leaf. I feel hopeful. I'm doing well.

His response comes quickly.

> Great! Does that mean you'll come back and work with us again?

I type my answer.

> I don't think so. Working there was one of the most memorable and wonderful experiences of my life. But I feel like it's time for me to move on to other things. I really appreciate everything you've done for me.

A longer pause this time before his reply comes in.

> I thought you'd be happy. How'd your talk with Mario go?

> It went great.

No response.

I imagine him sitting on the other end, unsure of what to make of me. They all thought they could win me back with a job. A job they so brutally took from me without considering for a second what it would do to me.

But I'm not angry anymore. I forgive them because losing that job led me here—to where I need to be. To my destiny.

Finally, his response comes through.

> Can we meet and talk?

Shaking my head with disbelief, I tap out my final reply.

> Goodbye, Drake.

I meant what I'd said. I do appreciate everything Drake did for me. He led me to Mario and the ability to expose Ricky Star. For that, I'll always be grateful. But I have bigger and better things to focus on now.

I glance at the clock. Time is ticking away, and I have errands to run for a big meeting ahead. And I need to be fully prepared. *Locked and loaded.*

CHAPTER FORTY-SIX

AFTER FLUFFING MY BLONDE WIG, I adjust my new fedora and tilt it to the left. The large sunglasses cover more than half of my face, rendering me practically unrecognizable. My outfit of black denim, a black sweater, and black knee-high boots complete the look. *I'm ready.*

After tossing my old clothes that I'd stuffed into a plastic bag into the garbage bin, I smack my crimson lips in the mirror and exit the restroom of the Cosmopolitan, heading straight for the escalator down to the main floor.

In my mind, I tell myself I'm powerful, invincible, and ready to make my mark. But the truth is, I'm nervous and more than I thought I'd be. *A lot more.* My plan relies on Mario to uphold his end of the deal. If this is going to work, I have to trust him. He said he would do it, and I have to believe him. He knows that if he doesn't come through, I can ruin him just as easily as I can ruin Ricky. But I really don't want to do that. I hope Mario understands that. *I need him to understand.*

Down the escalator, I stroll confidently past the chime of the slot machines and head out to go next door to the Bellagio. Striding down the Strip, I turn left to climb the escalator up to the pedestrian bridge to enter the glitzy hotel and casino, pausing only momentarily to admire the spectacular fountains.

Inside the doors of the Bellagio, I keep my head down, trying to blend into the crowd. My goal is to expose a predator, but I have no desire to be caught or for anyone to know I am behind Ricky's dethroning.

Working in the shadows, I can make the biggest impact and, more importantly, not be stopped. I don't want to sit in endless interviews with police officers or FBI agents. That will only slow me down and possibly silence me and the victims.

For the task, I've shaped a new persona—a mix of Rochelle and Jess. I like to think the courage inside me is partly hers. She gave me something all those years ago that I hadn't had in the thirteen years before I met her, a sense of belonging. It was then, for the first time in my life, I had been loved, cared for, and free from judgment. That kind of connection is rare—I know that now—and I miss it every single day.

I've spent years trying to fill that void, searching in all the wrong places: men, marriage, jobs, cars. I've tried so hard to fit in on the outside while on the inside I still felt achingly alone. I wish Rochelle was with me now. She can't be. But I like to think she is here with me in her own way.

After a sharp inhale, I keep on task, ignoring the glass flowers and marching toward the elevators. With no one else waiting, I press the up button with my knuckle and stare at the screen of my phone while I wait.

A moment later, the familiar ding of the doors opening sounds and I step inside, feeling lucky there is no one else taking the elevator at that moment.

On the way up, I tell myself I can *and* will do it. Not only do it, I'll nail it, and he'll be ruined forever.

The doors open on his floor, and I exit the elevator. My

nerves feel electric as I walk down the hallway. The corridor seems endless, but soon I see it—his room.

My heart hammers in my chest as I approach the door. I knock, my hand shaking slightly.

A few moments later, the door opens, and there stands Mario. His face is twisted with confusion as he looks me up and down.

"It's me," I whisper, and then remove my giant sunglasses, revealing a heavy, smoky eye. He seems puzzled, but before he can say anything, I say, "It's better this way."

He hesitates for a moment, then steps aside, waving me in.

Once I'm inside, Mario shuts the door behind him, and I pull a pair of tinted reading glasses from my purse to try to hide my identity. Between the hair, make-up, and glasses, there's a decent chance Ricky won't recognize me.

My stomach churns as my eyes land on him—the man who stole Rochelle's innocence. Ricky is lounging casually in a plush chair wearing black velour pants and a matching sweatshirt.

I glance back at Mario as he plants himself near the bar. He taps the edge of a planter, where he was supposed to have hidden a listening device. That was his part of the deal. He would plant the bug and get me alone with Ricky so I can confront him. We've had some phone calls over the last few days to make sure the details were perfect.

Mario clears his throat. "Ricky, this is Vanessa Jasper with the Vegas Voice."

Ricky's gaze flicks to me, his dark eyes scanning me from head to toe. He stands, extending a hand. "Hi there."

"Nice to meet you," I say, forcing a flirty smile as I shake his dry hand.

"You too," he says smoothly, gesturing to the sofa. "Please, have a seat."

I sit down on the sofa while he settles back into his chair.

Mario has set up the ruse that I'm a journalist looking to tell Ricky's side of the story—a ploy to cast *him* as the victim. As if anyone would believe that.

I reach into my bag and pull out a recorder, placing it on the table between us. "Do you mind if I record the interview?"

Ricky shrugs, his indifference grating. "Go ahead."

The recorder is my backup. If Mario's listening device doesn't work, or if he didn't plant it at all, I will still get what I came for.

"Thank you for agreeing to meet with me, Ricky."

"I want to get my side of the story out there."

"Great," I say, flipping open a notebook. "Let's jump right into it, shall we?"

"Yes, let's," he says, studying me carefully.

For a moment, I wonder if he recognizes me, but I push the thought aside and tip my head, concentrating on my notepad. "Let's start with one of the early allegations against you, from a post in the Facebook group, *Justice for Ricky Star's Victims*. This happened in 2005. There was a fifteen-year-old girl named Rochelle. She and her best friend, Jessica, approached you after a concert. They said they were hanging around the stage after a show when you offered to take them backstage to meet the New Soundz. Do you remember this incident?" *I'd redact the names from the recording later.*

"I don't remember names, but there were times when I brought girls backstage to meet the band. It was something nice I did for some of the New Soundz' biggest fans."

"In this particular instance, you left one of the girls, Jessica, sitting on a couch backstage while you took Rochelle, the fifteen-year-old blonde, with you. You told her you were going to check if the band was still around. You were gone for twenty minutes. When you returned, Rochelle was crying. She later told Jessica that she'd been assaulted. After you returned with

Rochelle, you rushed them out. They never met the band. Do you recall this?"

Ricky frowns. "Not really. Like I said, I tried to help the girls who stuck around. You know, the ones with grit, who would do anything to meet the band. And I guess now, years later, this is coming back to bite me. They say no good deed goes unpunished."

Fury surges through me, hot and unstoppable. My hands clench into fists as I lean forward. "Is that so? Is that your version of events?"

"Yes, it is. What other version is there?"

"Do you remember any of the girls? Do you remember Rochelle? She was fifteen years old, crying backstage!"

Ricky shrugs. "Sure, there were a few tears when the guys had already left. But I certainly didn't do anything inappropriate with them."

"Why would you leave one girl in the waiting area and take the other somewhere alone? That doesn't make any sense, does it?"

"No, I don't think I ever separated them. That doesn't make sense. That allegation is false."

He sits there, calm and calculated, denying everything. The anger inside me bubbles over—uncontainable. I shoot to my feet, shaking with fury. "It is not just an allegation! I am Jessica. I was there! I know what you did to Rochelle! She was only fifteen years old!"

Ricky's face drains of color as he jumps out of his chair. "What is this?" He turns toward Mario, who stands frozen in the corner of the suite. "Who is this woman you brought in here?"

Mario doesn't say a word.

"Look at me!" I shout, my voice cracking with anger. "He won't say anything because he knows! He knows exactly who you are. You've blackmailed him all these years because you're scum—a predator, a monster. You laughed at a fifteen-year-old girl after you destroyed her! And I'm sure she wasn't the first. She certainly wasn't the last! Admit it!"

Ricky's face twists with anger. "Get out of my hotel room! I'm not putting up with this!"

I pull Ricky's gun from my bag, and I aim it at him. "I'm not going anywhere and neither are you!" My body shakes, but I have trained for this. I know how to shoot the gun and hit my target, but that's not why I brought the gun. I hoped it would scare him into confessing. "Sit back down," I demand. To Mario, I say, "Stay where you are."

Mario's eyes are wide, but he nods in agreement.

Ricky's face is red, and his hands are curled into fists as he trudges back to the chair. He stands as if deciding what to do. I wave the gun at him. "Sit."

"What do you want from me?"

"I want you to admit what you did to Rochelle. You raped her. And you destroyed her!"

He sneers. "I didn't do anything to that girl."

"Yes, you did! You destroyed a fifteen-year-old girl! First you took her innocence and then you destroyed her sense of self and her sense of security and lastly her reason for living. You *killed* her!"

"I didn't kill *anyone*."

"You did! You killed her! After you did what you did, she was no longer herself." Hot tears stream down my face as the memories flood me. Snapping back to now, I focus the gun on Ricky. "She was so depressed. She felt worthless. Hopeless. You did that!"

He sits in silence. Not denying it.

"She struggled so hard. Her parents put her in therapy, and

they put her on antidepressants. None of it helped." I shake my head. "None of it helped!"

My body slumps as I mumble, "Rochelle killed herself because of what you did to her."

And in that moment, my mind shifts back to that last awful day. Rochelle finally called me back, I'd been so happy to hear from her, but after I said, "Hi, Rochelle!", in a low voice, she said, "Hey, Jess. I can't talk for long, but I wanted to say goodbye."

Filled with panic, I interrupted her. "What do you mean goodbye?" She didn't answer. My heart pounding, I asked again. "Rochelle, what do you mean?"

Her muffled cries came through the speaker as she said, "I can't do it anymore, Jess. I can't keep on like this. It has to end."

"But I'm here! We can get through this together!"

"I can't. I'm so sorry, Jess."

Frantically, I pleaded, "I need you! Please don't go!"

"I'm so sorry." She paused and then sang quietly, "I'll *always* love you."

All I could say was, "Please don't go!" over and over until my final cries were met with a click. She'd hung up and I never saw her or heard her voice again.

Her mother called me the next morning to tell me they had found her. She'd taken too many pills. She was gone. And that day, part of me died too.

Sudden movement throws me back to the present, and Ricky is out of the chair, reaching for the gun. I refuse to let it go, and the next thing I know, there is a sound like a firecracker in my ear and a thud as Ricky crumples to the floor.

CHAPTER FORTY-SEVEN

MARIO

Blood pools beneath his crumpled body. For a moment, everything is still—except for the pounding in my ears. I stand frozen, staring, unable to process what has just happened. Jess nudges him with her boot and steps back. Her body is stiff, but I can see her hands are shaking, the weapon still in her grip.

"Jess!" I gasp, taking a step toward her.

She looks at me. Her face is a mask of horror with streaks of black mascara and tears. Her wide eyes lock onto mine, unblinking, as though even she can't believe what she's done.

She flinches, her gaze darting back to the lifeless body on the floor. Her lips quiver before she speaks, her voice trembling. "I didn't mean to. He... he tried to grab it. I didn't mean to."

I nod slowly, trying to steady myself. "It's okay, Jess," I say gently, taking another cautious step toward her.

But as I move closer, Jess's demeanor shifts. Her hand tightens around the weapon, and her body tenses. She raises the weapon again, pointing it at me.

"Don't move!"

My heart pounds so hard it feels like it might burst. I raise my hands slowly, trying to keep my voice calm. "Jess... it's okay. I'm not going to hurt you."

Her chest heaves as dark tears continue down her face. Her eyes dart between me and Ricky on the floor.

In that moment, I realize the full weight of what has happened. I've underestimated her and underestimated the fragility of her mind. I've made a terrible, terrible mistake. And now, I fear that I may pay for it with my life.

CHAPTER FORTY-EIGHT

Mario stares at me, his face pale and his eyes filled with terror. He is part of the New Soundz. The band and the community I love. The thought makes my grip on the gun falter and my body slumps. I didn't even truly want to shoot Ricky. Not that I feel bad he is gone. He deserved it. But what will happen next? Jail. A trial. Will I survive it?

I've never done something like this before. It is my first... murder. My breath hitches at the word. Can I get a good attorney? Maybe plead down to lesser charges? It happens all the time with people who have privilege. But then again, sometimes they throw the book at people like me—people who don't have the right connections or enough power to shield themselves.

Maybe the press will be on my side. He is a predator, after all. If they know my story, they might even let me off. But that is a long shot. I can't take that chance. My work *isn't* finished.

Mario looks petrified. I guess I would be too if someone was pointing a gun at my face. Knowing there is no way I can shoot him, I lower the weapon.

"I'm so sorry. I didn't mean to do it."

The words feel hollow as they leave my lips. *What's done is done*. I can't kill Mario. I love all the New Soundz. They've never done anything to me. And even though I stopped going to their concerts and stopped listening to their music all those years ago, it's only because of what happened to Rochelle. That was Ricky's fault, not Mario's.

But Mario has known. He has known what Ricky was doing. If he'd spoken up, maybe Rochelle would have been saved. But then again, if Mario had told anyone, it would've ruined all of them. But was that more important than Rochelle's life? *No*. Was Mario just as responsible? If that were true, I guess I was responsible for anyone who was assaulted by Ricky after Rochelle—I hadn't said anything either.

"Why don't you give me the gun?"

I shake my head. "I don't know what to do, Mario. I'm so scared." Scared of prison and afraid of what I am capable of. I can feel the tears flowing and everything blurs together—Mario's face, the room around us, the sound of my own heartbeat. I am losing control again.

"It'll be OK, Jess.... But we need to act fast here."

Time is slipping away, and the gunshot might have already drawn someone's attention. Someone could come after me. They could be here any second.

"I'm going to go to jail, Mario," I say. "This was supposed to be the beginning of something bigger, something better. But I failed Rochelle."

"No, you didn't, Jess. You stopped a predator. You stopped him from hurting anybody else. You stopped him from getting away with what he did to all those women. I know it, and you know it."

I stare at him. "But was it worth it? He never admitted anything. If I go to jail, my life is over. I thought my life was just beginning."

Mario's eyes dart to the gun still in my hand. He reaches out hesitantly, but I pull back, raising it slightly. "Stay... stay there, Mario. I just—I need to think this through."

It feels like my whole life is playing on a loop in my mind—every failure, every moment of loss. Childhood memories of abandonment, neglect, and loneliness. Meeting Rochelle and finally feeling like I belonged somewhere. Then losing her. Trying to rebuild, getting married, then my husband leaving me. Being assaulted by Sam. Thinking I'd found a fresh start in Vegas, only to be fired and have the New Soundz ripped away from me.

And now I've killed someone.

"I don't know what to do, Mario. I don't want to go to jail."

Mario shakes his head firmly. "We don't have a lot of time, Jess. Let's think about this logically. You don't even look like yourself. Surveillance footage? It's just a blonde woman in a hat with glasses covering most of your face. There's no evidence. You've been careful."

He is right. I have been careful. There is no video of me leaving the hotel as myself. I've entered the Bellagio in disguise. All I need to do is leave and go into a nearby casino's restroom, take off the hat, glasses, and wig—no one can recognize me.

But what about Mario? What will happen to him? Could he be dragged into this too? Will he turn me in? My thoughts spiral, and almost involuntarily, my arm begins to raise the gun again.

"I don't know, Mario."

"Would it help to talk about Rochelle? She sounds like she meant a lot to you."

"She was my everything. My only true best friend. The first time I ever belonged to someone. We had each other... and then she was gone. She was taken from me. Maybe I don't have anything left to lose."

I glance down at the gun in my hand and realize I have options.

Mario steps forward, slowly this time, and places his hand gently on my shoulder. I look up at him, my breath hitching. His eyes are steady on mine. "It's okay. I'll help you."

CHAPTER FORTY-NINE

MARIO

IF I WASN'T PANICKED BEFORE, I certainly am now. I don't think she's going to turn the gun on me, but I can see it in her eyes—she might turn it on herself. Everything I've learned about Jess tells me she has loved deeply and has been hurt just as deeply. And I am part of that pain.

I've covered up for Ricky for years. Maybe if I'd spoken out earlier, her friend would never have been hurt. Rochelle might still be alive. But I've kept his secrets for so long, and now Jess is unraveling right in front of me. She hasn't admitted it outright, but I know she is the one who has exposed him. The Facebook group that allowed women to come forward with their stories and get some closure—I know it is all her doing.

"If you just go, I'll say I didn't see you. I'll come up with a story, okay? I'll lie to the police."

Jess blinks, her hands shaking as she clutches the gun tighter.

I continue, "I've been hiding things for a long time. I should've said something all those years ago about Ricky. I'm so sorry that I didn't. But as you can see, I'm good at keeping secrets. I kept his for decades. The least I can do is keep yours.

Get out of here. Get rid of the gun. I'll say some woman came in —maybe one of his victims—I don't know. I'll tell them I'd never seen her before, and she left just before anyone called in about the gunshot. I've got you. I swear. But you have to hurry."

She hesitates, staring at me, her eyes filled with desperation.

"I know you loved Rochelle. I know you love the New Soundz, too. Fans like you gave us a wonderful life. And the rest of the guys... they're also so grateful for everything we got to do because of you. You were part of that. Let me do this. I swear I'll help. Get rid of the gun. Get out of here."

Her breathing slows as my words begin to sink in. Still holding the gun, she glances down at her bag, then back at me. "You'd really do that for me?"

"It's the least I can do. Please, just go before it's too late."

Jess looks at me for a long moment before nodding. She tucks the gun into her purse and steps closer. "What about the device in the planter?"

I almost forgot. I hurry over and pull the recorder from the planter and hand it to Jess. "Go now."

She nods again, takes a deep breath, and walks toward the door. As it closes behind her, I think, *Saving Jess is the very least I can do.*

CHAPTER FIFTY

WITH MY SUNGLASSES BACK ON, I rush down the hall, my heart pounding so loudly it drowns out every other sound. At the bank of elevators, I press the down button with my elbow, careful not to leave fingerprints. When the elevator doors open almost immediately, I freeze for a moment. Is it a sign? The universe is on my side? I don't know. All I know is that I have to move.

Inside, the elevator is empty—thank goodness. I step in quickly, keeping my head down, and use my elbow again to press the button for the lobby. Cameras are everywhere, watching my every move. I can't risk giving them a clear shot of me.

If Mario sticks to his word and doesn't tell anyone it was me, maybe I'll be okay. I haven't touched anything. The gun is still with me, and I hold all the recordings. I have to believe in something, and I choose to believe in Mario—I have no other choice. And I choose to believe in the New Soundz because, after all these years, they've never let me down. Although the shock that Mario knew Ricky's true nature threw me for a loop, and when I thought he'd had me fired, I wasn't sure how to feel. But when he came to me and apologized and got my job back, I knew his true nature. He is a good man. And as I flee, I know he'll keep his word. *I hope.*

There is so much more I want to say to him, so much I want to explain. But he is right—I can't stay. I have to get out of here, and quickly.

The elevator dings, pulling me out of my thoughts. The doors slide open, revealing an empty space. Another sign that the universe is guiding me. I adjust my sweater, tuck my chin, and exit.

When I reach the lobby, I step into the crowd. My heart races, but I don't look back.

I have to keep moving.

I leave the Bellagio through the front entrance, where the cars line the driveway. I hurry down the steps and cross the street with my head down. I have to keep moving, blend in, and get to safety.

After crossing the street, I duck into the Paris Hotel and Casino, slipping through the revolving doors as if I belong there. The glittering chandeliers and buzzing slot machines create a surreal contrast to the panic inside me. I know where the restrooms are—tucked toward the back near the shops. I can change my appearance there, maybe even buy a sparkly top from one of the boutiques on my way out.

I'll pack up my things from my suite and figure out a way to get rid of the gun. I have to leave Vegas. Probably forever.

Where will I go?

The thought hits me like a brick, but I push it aside. I can't worry about that now. First, I have to disappear, but the airport isn't an option yet. Not until I get rid of the gun and recorders.

Lake Mead.

The original plan. I'll get a car. Pay cash. Drive to the lake and toss the gun. Afterward, I can hit the open road. I can go anywhere, maybe drive to an airport in California and go somewhere tropical, somewhere happy—just for a little while.

The thought twists something in my chest. I won't even get to see the New Soundz perform on opening night. I've seen them during the dress rehearsal, but the show would be different—electrified with thousands of screaming fans. Leaving them like this feels like leaving a piece of myself behind. But I have no choice.

I have to do what I have to do.

The restroom is quiet when I enter. I slip into a stall, locking the door behind me. The wig comes off first, and I fluff out my hair, running my fingers through it until it falls into place. Next, the sweater. I pull it off, leaving me in a simple tank top, jeans, and boots. I glance down at the boots and freeze.

Blood.

There is blood on the tip of my right boot.

"Oh no," I mutter under my breath. I grab toilet paper from the roll and furiously wipe at the leather, scrubbing until the red smear is gone. My hands quiver as I clean, and I realize I'll have to dump the boots too.

Once the blood is gone, I step out of the stall and stare at myself in the mirror. My reflection is... horrifying. I look like a reject from the band Kiss. I grab paper towels and turn on the faucet, then scrub off the black streaks from my cheeks. Then I try to remove all of the eye makeup. It won't all come off with just water but at least I now look less like I'm wearing a Halloween costume and more like a pale raccoon. *Good enough*.

As I hurry out of the restroom, a thought echoes in my mind. Can I really get away with murder?

CHAPTER FIFTY-ONE

Inside my new room at the Horseshoe Hotel and Casino, I sit in the chair by the window, staring out at the bright lights of the Strip. From here, I have a perfect view of the Sphere. Its enormous digital surface is lit up with a giant smiley face. For a moment, I let myself wonder—Is it a message? Don't worry, be happy?

I've cleared out my suite, leaving no trace but not checking out yet. I don't want a record of me leaving right after Ricky's death. There are so many things that could go wrong, leading me right into a jail cell. Worry is all I have done for the past two days while holed up with only provisions from Walgreens.

Two days since the shooting. Two days of compulsively checking online for any news about what has happened. So far, there has been nothing. No breaking stories, no whispers of an investigation—just silence.

It feels peculiar, almost ominous. Maybe they are waiting for official statements. Someone from Ricky's legal team. A spokesperson from the New Soundz.

Mario hasn't contacted me since I fled.

No news is good news, right?

I return to my laptop, the screen glowing faintly in the dim room. I hesitate for a moment, then type his name into the search bar. My fingers hover over the keyboard as I hit Enter.

The page loads, and I gasp. There it is—not plastered across every headline, but enough to make the front page of Google News.

"Tour Manager for the New Soundz—Ricky Star—Accused Predator, Shot Dead in Hotel Room in Las Vegas."

I click the article. The words swim in front of me, but I force myself to focus.

"A spokesperson for Ricky Star's team confirmed that the disgraced tour manager, a legend with over thirty years in the music industry, was shot and killed in his Las Vegas hotel room late Tuesday night. No suspects have been identified at this time, but authorities state the investigation is ongoing and all leads are being pursued."

I sit back in my chair, relieved. No suspects. *Yet*.

The words roll through my mind, over and over. My grip on the armrests tightens as I reread the article. They don't have anything. No trail. No clues pointing to me. At least, not yet. I need to keep it that way.

For the first time in two days, I exhale deeply and lean back against the chair. The glow of the Sphere outside fills the room with a faint, surreal light. Maybe, just maybe, I've pulled this off—thanks to Mario. But I know better than to think this is all over—not yet. There is still the matter of evidence that needs to be destroyed.

CHAPTER FIFTY-TWO

MARIO

The homicide detective says, "Thank you for coming down to the station, Mario. We really appreciate it."

"No problem. Anything I can do to help."

Truth be told, I've never been inside a police station before —not to be questioned, anyway. The sterile walls and the faint smell of coffee mixed with stress make me uncomfortable. This isn't a place I want to be, but I've known it was inevitable. After all, I was the one who called 911 to report Ricky's death.

The detective says, "Why don't you start from the beginning? What were you doing in Ricky's hotel room? Why were you meeting with him?"

Before I'd come out, life had always felt like a performance —an act to fit in. I thought I'd left that behind, but now? Now I had to step back into that role because I meant what I'd said to Jess, and I hoped she'd taken my advice, destroyed the evidence, and laid low. I am doing my part, and I need her to do hers because the last thing I need is to be accused of being involved in a coverup. From what my lawyer told me, the offense comes with jail time. Jess and I are in this together.

Not only that but this is my chance to make something right

out of the wrong I've been living with for far too long. I've kept Ricky's secrets and now I can only hope Jess will keep mine. We are bonded in a way that feels strange, considering we barely know each other. We only worked together briefly, but now we share a secret—one of a criminal nature. She trusted me to have her back, and now I have to trust her not to reveal that I knew about Ricky Star and all his offenses. I can't let that get out—not now, not ever.

Continuing one of the biggest performances of my life, I say, "Ricky asked me to meet him at his hotel room. We've been friends for over twenty years, and with everything that was happening—the news, the accusations—he was... struggling. He needed someone to talk to."

"He just wanted to talk?"

"Yeah. He seemed overwhelmed with everything in the media. I guess he was looking for support."

The detective scribbles something in his notebook, but I keep my expression steady. They'd already questioned me at the scene, but then they'd asked for a second interview. My lawyer assured me this was normal—routine, even. They interviewed witnesses and suspects multiple times to see if any new memories surfaced or if stories changed. I know this is a test, but I'm ready. I've rehearsed my story, and I am not going to slip up.

Still, the weight of the truth presses down on me. For decades, I've been complicit in Ricky's crime. I protected him by saying nothing. Now I am protecting someone else, and it isn't just Jess I am shielding. It is myself, too.

"He said he was getting nervous that he might go to jail or be completely ostracized from the business. He wanted my advice."

The detective tilts his head, pen poised over his notebook. "Why did he ask you specifically for advice and not his lawyer or PR team?"

I hesitate for half a beat, then say, "We bonded back in the day. He knew that I was gay back then, and he kept it quiet when I still had to play the part of the straight, female-loving boy band member. I had his back, and he had mine."

The detective nods slowly. "All right. So, you were having a conversation. What time did you say you got there?"

"Around six PM. I don't know the exact time."

"What happened when you arrived?"

"We talked. Had a drink."

"What did you drink?"

"Whiskey neat. Both of us."

"What did you talk about?"

"He was telling me about some of the allegations."

"And then what happened?"

"Someone knocked on the door."

"What time?"

I swallow. This is it—the part I've rehearsed over and over. "I don't know, maybe seven. I asked Ricky if he was expecting anyone, and he said no. He told me he hadn't been answering the door at all—not even for housekeeping—because he was afraid it might be paparazzi or someone trying to ask him about the accusations."

"But you answered the door?"

"I did."

"And what happened?"

I keep my voice even, steady. "I opened the door, and it was a woman. I don't know—maybe 5'5"? Blonde hair, wearing black clothes and sunglasses. A hat."

"Did you know the woman?"

"No. I'd never seen her before. At least, not that I remember."

I practiced that answer endlessly, rehearsing it in front of the mirror until it sounded natural. My husband walked in on me once, talking to myself, and asked what I was doing. He thought I was losing it. But I told him I was just rehearsing for when I meet fans at the meet-and-greets before the opening of the shows. He believed me. I didn't want to lie to him, but I couldn't tell him what I had done and what I'd been a part of.

"And then what happened?"

"I asked her why she was there, but before I could answer, she pushed her way past me. I was surprised but didn't think too much of it. I closed the door behind her, assuming she knew Ricky." I paused for effect, glancing down briefly before continuing. "She started talking to him—then yelling at him."

"Yelling?"

"She was calling him a pig, a predator. Saying that he'd hurt her and that he had to pay. She kept repeating it—he had to pay for what he did to her."

"And how did Ricky respond?"

"He said he didn't know who she was. He kept insisting he didn't hurt anybody and that she was crazy. But when he tried to push her out, she pulled out a gun, they struggled a bit, and she shot him."

"How many times did she shoot him?"

"Just once."

The detective writes in his notebook again before looking back up at me, his expression unreadable. I force myself to hold his gaze, even as my heart thuds in my chest.

"What happened after that?"

"She looked down at him like she was surprised at what she'd done. Then she looked at me and pointed the gun at me. I begged her not to shoot me, too. I begged for my life."

"And?"

"She hesitated," I say, my voice faltering just enough to sound genuine, but considering it had happened, it was easy.

"She said she couldn't have any witnesses. She told me she was sorry, but... but she'd have to kill me too."

The detective's expression didn't change. "So, why didn't she?"

"I begged her," I repeat. "I told her I have a son at home. I pleaded with her. She waited for what felt like forever before finally telling me to go to the bedroom. She said if I came out before five minutes were up, she'd shoot me. So, I went. I stayed in the bedroom, terrified she might come back to kill me. As soon as the five minutes were up, I called 911."

"And you'd never seen this woman before?"

"Not that I can remember. I've met a lot of people, as you can imagine, but I didn't recognize her."

The detective takes a few more notes, the sound of his pen scratching against the paper unnervingly loud. I shift in my seat, uncomfortable in the silence.

I know why they are questioning me a second time. They are looking for cracks, inconsistencies. But there shouldn't be any.

The truth was that, shortly after I called 911, I called my lawyer. He talked me through exactly what to say, down to every detail and what to expect going forward. My lawyer asked if I was leaving anything out, as if he could tell I was omitting a few key details. I simply stated, "Not that I can say." As soon as Jess left the room, I'd begun rewriting the script in my mind, tightening it, making it more believable. A better story. My lawyer picked up on the fact I wasn't planning to say another thing about it, and then he explained that, moving forward, I couldn't change a single detail of my story. Not to the police, not to anyone.

The detective finally closes his notebook and looks back at me. "Thank you for coming down, Mario. We really appreciate it."

"No problem," I say, standing up. "Anything I can do to help. I want them to catch who did this. Ricky didn't deserve that." I lower my head, letting an expression of grief cross my face. It isn't hard to summon. The weight of everything—the lies, the secrets, the past—presses down on me, and I feel myself bowing under it.

The detective hands me a card. "If you think of anything else, give us a call."

"Of course," I say, tucking the card into my pocket.

As I leave the station, I let out a long breath. Another interview down. How many more to go? It doesn't matter. My story won't change. I've made my peace with it, and I only hope it helps Jess and the women Ricky hurt find some peace too.

CHAPTER FIFTY-THREE

ONE YEAR LATER

THE SUN SHINES down as I walk through the cemetery, the warmth on my face contrasting with the heaviness in my heart. A year has passed since Ricky's death—a year since I fled Las Vegas, leaving behind a part of myself and an entire chapter of my life.

I haven't heard from Mario since that night, nor has the Las Vegas Police Department contacted me, not that I'm easy to find. I know there is the possibility I could still be caught despite the careful planning, and of course, there is the possibility Mario could tell the truth about that night, and I'll be in handcuffs.

The latest reports say Ricky's case has gone cold. That is both a relief and a quiet terror. I know the status could change at any moment.

I keep up with the *Justice for Ricky Star's Victims* Facebook page, scrolling through posts and comments from women like Rochelle. Some celebrate that Ricky is gone, writing that they finally feel a sense of peace. Others speculate about who did it, fantasizing about throwing a party for the person responsible.

It feels surreal. It's strange how life twists and turns, dropping you in places you'd never imagine.

I haven't met any of the women in person, but online, we are a force. The community is strong, even after Ricky's death. Every day, more women continue to come forward with their stories. There will never be a trial, no moment in court to face the man who hurt them, but their monster is dead and buried.

And in that, I take comfort.

It's all I have left.

I can't return to my old life in California or associate with my friends or my mom and sister. After the shooting, I didn't return text messages or voicemails. I hope they're not worrying. Soon, I'll send some cryptic messages that I'm okay—messages that won't reveal my location. I fear if I hadn't made the break, my new home would be a jail cell, so I've started over as someone new in a new town where nobody knows who I am.

To keep myself busy in the real world, and make some money, I now work in a coffee shop. What began as a way to make ends meet has turned into something more. And like my time with the New Soundz, I find joy in the simplicity of it—getting to know regulars, chatting with strangers, becoming part of the neighborhood. It isn't flashy or lucrative, but it's everything I never realized I needed.

I have community, on and offline. The Facebook group has already had a few suggestions that we should take on other predators and expose them for their deeds. I agree wholeheartedly. We've already chosen our next target... but enough about that. Today is about Rochelle.

Back in California for the first time since I left for Vegas, I make my way to her grave, a bouquet of pink peonies in one hand and a New Soundz button in the other. When I reach her marker, I pause, my breath catching as I read her name etched into the stone.

I haven't been here since the funeral. For so long, I couldn't bear it. If I didn't visit, I could pretend she was still alive—off in another city or away at college. But her grave makes it real.

I kneel, placing the bouquet and the button in the holder, and then I sit cross-legged on the grass. Slowly, I rest my hand on the stone, letting its coolness ground me.

"We got him, Rochelle. He's never going to hurt anyone ever again."

The words hang in the air, their weight sinking into me. For the first time, I feel like I can breathe.

I begin talking to her, the way I used to when we were inseparable. I tell her about Vegas, about what I've seen and done, about how incredible the New Soundz are in person. But I don't stop there—I tell her about the life I've rebuilt since leaving, about the women who keep sharing their stories online, and about the future I am finally starting to imagine for myself. Ricky Star is only one predator in a sea of monsters. There are many others who need to be stopped, and I am determined to do just that.

Finally, I lean forward, plant a kiss on the cold stone, and sing in a low voice, "I will *always* love you."

And I will.

From the day we met as kids, we'd been linked. Two sides of the same coin. Her fight has become my fight, and the loss of her nearly ended me too. But Rochelle has also given me a purpose, and as I embark on my next mission, I know she will be with me every step of the way.

THANK YOU!

Thank you for reading *Please Don't Go*. I hope you enjoyed reading it as much as I loved writing it. If you did, I would greatly appreciate if you could post a short review.

Reviews are crucial for any author and can make a huge difference in visibility of current and future works. Reviews allow us to continue doing what we love, *writing stories*. Not to mention, I would be forever grateful!

Thank you!

ALSO BY H.K. CHRISTIE

The Martina Monroe Series —a nail-biting crime thriller series starring PI Martina Monroe and her unofficial partner Detective August Hirsch of the Cold Case Squad. If you like high-stakes games, jaw-dropping twists, and suspense that will keep you on the edge of your seat, then you'll love the Martina Monroe crime thriller series.

The Val Costa Series —a gripping crime thriller with heart-pounding suspense. If you love Martina, you'll love Val.

The Neighbor Two Doors Down —a dark and witty psychological thriller. If you like unpredictable twists, page-turning suspense, and unreliable narrators, then you'll love *The Neighbor Two Doors Down*.

The Selena Bailey Series (1 - 5) —a suspenseful series featuring a young Selena Bailey and her turbulent path to becoming a top-notch private investigator as led by her mentor, Martina Monroe.

A Permanent Mark A heartless killer. Weeks without answers. Can she move on when a murderer walks free? If you like riveting suspense and gripping mysteries, then you'll love *A Permanent Mark* - starring a grown up Selena Bailey.

For H.K. Christie's full catalog go to: **www.authorhkchristie.com**

At **www.authorhkchristie.com** you can also sign up for the H.K. Christie reader club where you'll be the first to hear about upcoming novels, new releases, giveaways, promotions, and a **free e-copy of the prequel to the Martina Monroe Thriller Series, *Crashing Down*!**

ABOUT THE AUTHOR

H. K. Christie watched horror films far too early in life. Inspired by the likes of Stephen King, Jodi Picoult, true crime podcasts, and a vivid imagination she now writes suspenseful thrillers.

She found her passion for writing when she embarked on a one-woman habit breaking experiment. Although she didn't break her habit she did discover a love of writing and has been at it ever since.

When not working on her latest novel, H.K. Christie can be found eating & drinking with friends, walking around the lakes, or playing with her favorite furry pal.

She is a native and current resident of the San Francisco Bay Area.

To learn more about H.K. Christie and her books, or simply to say, "hello", go to **www.authorhkchristie.com**.

At **www.authorhkchristie.com** you can also sign up for the H.K. Christie reader club where you'll be the first to hear about upcoming novels, new releases, giveaways, promotions, and a free e-copy of the prequel to the Martina Monroe Thriller Series, *Crashing Down!*

ACKNOWLEDGMENTS

Heartfelt thanks to my incredible Advanced Reader Team—your sharp eyes, honest feedback, and enthusiastic support mean the world to me. Your early reads and thoughtful reviews help bring these stories to life.

To my editor, Paula Lester—thank you for your keen insight and careful edits, and to Ryan Mahan, my eagle-eyed proofreader, for catching those last lingering typos. I'm so grateful to have you both on my team.

To Odile, my brilliant cover designer—thank you for your creativity, vision, and guidance in capturing the perfect visual for each book.

To my writing companion and self-appointed supervisor, Charlie—thank you for your steady gaze, your timely nudges for snack breaks, and your unwavering belief that a good walk can solve just about anything. You keep me grounded and moving forward.

To the mister—your love and encouragement are my constant anchor. Thank you for always cheering me on.

To Danny, Donnie, Joe, Jon, and Jordan—thank you for the years of music, magic, and comfort. During one of the hardest times in my life, your songs and performances gave me a place to escape, a reason to smile, and something positive to hold on to. I'll see you in Las Vegas.

And finally, to my readers—you are the reason I get to do what I love every single day. Thank you for joining me on these dark, twisty journeys and for making this dream a reality.

www.ingramcontent.com/pod-product-compliance
Lightning Source LLC
Chambersburg PA
CBHW031057080625
27887CB00018B/140